LIGHTNING ENCOUNTER

Anne Saunders

CHIVERS
THORNDIKE

This Large Print book is published by BBC Audiobooks Ltd, Bath, England and by Thorndike Press®, Waterville, Maine, USA.

Published in 2005 in the U.K. by arrangement with the author.

Published in 2005 in the U.S. by arrangement with Juliet Burton Literary Agency.

U.K. Hardcover ISBN 1–4056–3334–4 (Chivers Large Print)
U.K. Softcover   ISBN 1–4056–3335–2 (Camden Large Print)
U.S. Softcover   ISBN 0–7862–7633–9 (British Favorites)

Copyright © Anne Saunders 1971

The text of this Large Print edition is unabridged.
Other aspects of the book may vary from the original edition.

Set in 16 pt. New Times Roman.

Printed in Great Britain on acid-free paper.

British Library Cataloguing in Publication Data available

Library of Congress Cataloging-in-Publication Data

Saunders, Anne.
    Lightning encounter / by Anne Saunders.
       p.   cm.
    "Thorndike Press large print British favorites."—T.p. verso.
    ISBN 0–7862–7633–9 (lg. print : sc : alk. paper)
    1. Alienation (Social psychology)—Fiction. 2. England—Fiction.
3. Large type books. I. Title.
PR6069.A88L54 2005
813'.54—dc22   2005004928

CHAPTER ONE

The tempo of evening seemed to have caught the busy main street unawares; having rid itself of the bustling shopping public, it hadn't had time to recharge itself to meet the cinema going, entertainment seeking section of the community who thronged the pavement, hailed taxis, or hung in agonized indecision in totally inadequate shop doorways.

It wasn't a day for dawdling, unless you happened to be blessed with a huge umbrella. Sadly Karen wasn't. Instead she was lumbered with a suitcase, a tartan holdall and a capacious handbag. Which constituted her entire worldly possessions. Whenever she thought about it she felt like weeping, so she tried not to think about it very often. But this was difficult because she couldn't find a subject of thought that absorbed her to the exclusion of her present predicament.

She had only walked the one street from the railway station, but already she could feel the damp seeping through to her shoulders. She thought this perfectly matched her mood, which was a mixture of dejection and impatience. Yet she had only herself to blame for missing the train connection. She should have read the notice board before going into the buffet for a cup of tea. Funny thing was, she hadn't drunk the tea, just stared at it until it had grown cold. She must have wanted it, otherwise she wouldn't have ordered it, or could it be she yearned to be with people who had cut out of the dash and go and had time to sit awhile, perhaps even extend her a friendly smile.

As her suitcase bumped against her leg for the third time, she wondered why she hadn't thought to leave it in the left luggage place. It was bad enough to be impeded by the rain and the indifferent assortment of jostling elbows, without having to bear this self-inflicted torture.

The light from a steamed-up restaurant window attracted her eye, and on impulse she was pushing open the plate glass door; in her overburdened state she found it necessary to adopt a rear attack and fall in with the swing of the door. A lot of other people seemed to share the same idea, not her method of entry, but getting out of the rain to dally in an atmosphere that was pungent, friendly, warm.

All the tables were occupied and she was on the point of turning tail when a sympathetic waiter whispered in her ear: 'I can fit you in if you don't mind sharing.' She demurely said she didn't mind; she didn't tell him that she welcomed sharing, that a, 'Foul day!' or, 'Would you be kind enough to pass the salt?' would be scintillating conversation after a day spent travelling in gloomy silence. The lady occupying the seat next to hers on the plane coming over had looked the jolly type, but she had promptly buried herself in a book and hadn't looked up until the sign flashed to tell them to fasten their seat belts and prepare for landing.

The waiter adeptly led her to a corner table. Her feeling of anticipation and pleasure evaporated as she sighted her table companion. She would have preferred a cherubic fatherly type, with a round pink face and a manner of friendly benevolence. Not someone relatively young, around thirty-thirty-two and impeccably turned out. That brief impression was all she got because he used his menu like a shield to ward off her prying eyes.

Ian Nicholson didn't particularly want to share his table; he agreed because he was an accommodating sort of person and it didn't occur to him to do otherwise. Having made his choice he allowed the menu to slip an inch, and was unprepared for the collision of eyes. His were dark; someone once told him they were awesome at first appraisal because their unique colouring, practically jet, made them appear fierce and condemning. The same person had told him they went rather well with his granite jaw, flaring nose, and hair, only a shade lighter than those splendid eyes, rising thickly from a vee-shaped peak.

Hers were jewel green, edged with a double row of back curling lashes. He wondered if

3

they were really so green, or if it was her sun tan that enhanced and enriched the colour. Without them she would have been a nondescript as her features, though good, were too regular to make an impression. Yet he felt that if she released her mouth from its line of pinched tightness, allowing it to become mobile, the result might just be breathtaking.

Her hands made a feminine movement to her hair, pushing the ends up and away from her face, as if she was suddenly aware that the flattened, sorry little strands weren't looking their best. Or perhaps she didn't like rain water dripping down her turned-up collar to ice her skin.

He said: 'Dear me! You are wet.' She agreed that she was and for no apparent reason burst into a laugh, but one which lacked mirth and was a near relation to hysteria. He thought, if you were a kitten I'd mop you dry; she wasn't a kitten but it seemed such a good idea that he got out his handkerchief and proceeded to do just that. She accepted his ministrations as if she knew it was futile to protest and when he was satisfied that he'd removed as much excess moisture from her face and hair as he possibly could, he ordered her to remove her coat. At least it had the ring of an order, although he intended it to sound like a persuasive request. She had the look of one who'd amassed enough difficulties without adding a severe chill and all its attendant discomforts.

She was beginning to regard her coat as a liability, anyway, so she gratefully handed it over. He hung it near the radiator to dry off, and regarded her assets, which included a well defined waist, but it was really her legs that riveted his attention. They were superb and he was sorry when she sat down, tucking them out of sight.

At his insistence she ordered the soup. To warm her up and put a bit of colour in her cheeks. She laughed and touched her sun tan and he said all right, she looked as if she might be pale.

In gourmet style a bottle of wine sat beside his plate. He asked the waiter for a second glass, which he filled generously and handed to her.

'Drink it up,' he persuasively requested, although it still sounded like an order. When she didn't immediately respond he accused her of going coy on him. She replied that she was never coy and picked up the glass with such great deliberation that it was almost a flourish. After several sips the red wine began to take effect, her mouth lost its crippling numbness and grew attractively mobile. He felt immensely pleased with himself for seeing beyond the wrapping, for knowing about the elusive quality capable of transforming her from a misery-drowned kitten into a saucy, damned attractive girl.

'Now,' he said decisively. 'Perhaps you'd like to tell me all about it.'

'It?' she prevaricated.

He looked significantly at the luggage strewn haphazardly at her feet where she'd dropped it. 'Don't tell me you're out on a shopping spree.'

She appraised the suitcase and then hurriedly looked away, as if she found the sight of it distasteful.

They skirted glances, but his eyes had a drawing power she hadn't reckoned with. But she didn't want to talk, she did, but about the weather, no not the weather, that, like her predicament, was a damp line; but about the food, the wine, the flowers on the table, the people at the next table. Anything that was vital, exciting, alive. Anything that kept her mind occupied. And yet, confronted with such kindly persuasion, yes it was that now and not an order, she was tempted to succumb; but, she reminded herself sternly, young ladies of newly gained independence don't pour out their troubles to strangers, even though the eyes she had dubbed satanic had acquired a glimmer of kindness.

Besides, it all seemed so very far away, a medieval world away, and she could hardly relate herself to the girl who'd squandered the blue and gold days, thinking they would never run out. If she wanted to tell, she wouldn't know where to begin. With Angela? Even

6

though she did think the fair English girl in the bikini was not the beginning, but the end.

She'd fallen asleep while sunbathing, at a time when all sensible people were taking forty winks after lunch, or playing it safe sipping cooling drinks under shady beach umbrellas. Karen spotted her first. Tugging her father's arm she'd casually remarked: 'Somebody's going to wake up with more than a headache.'

'We'd better do something about it,' he agreed thoughtfully. 'Shall I tweak her nose, or tickle her toes?'

'Neither,' she said. 'I think our chatter has done the trick. She appears to be stirring.'

'Hello,' greeted the girl, sitting up to repentantly rub her eyes. 'Did I drop off? That was foolish of me, on my first day too!' She had very blue eyes, Karen noticed, and a long rope of golden hair. She wore, besides that eye catching bikini, a glazed and smitten look. Karen prepared to meet her father's amused glance, because in appearance he very much resembled a film star portraying a dashing buccaneer, and he was used to females behaving as if they'd had a spot too much sun at first meeting. And second meeting. There rarely followed a third. He'd wink at Karen and say: 'Time to pull up anchor, sprat.'

They didn't live on the mainland, but on a tiny island, one of the few not yet taken over, although the odd tourist had started to infiltrate, and once every two weeks they came

7

by boat, so that her father could sell his paintings. He was an artist, and in an area overrun with artists he was sufficient of his craft to make a comparatively good living. That is to say, if his paintings did not command a high price, they ate well because food was cheap and plentiful. Especially sea food which, luckily, they'd developed a taste for. Necessity had made Karen a versatile cook.

Anyway, on that day, which started her world toppling, the amused and kindly derision was smartly wiped off her face by the look on her father's. It was a look she had never seen there before and at first it was difficult to assess. With a slow awakening of thought she realized it was the exact counterpart of their look: the long string of females who'd danced vigil to his charms.

Her mother died when she was very young and although friends teased and prodded him, he showed not the slightest inclination to get back into double harness. He claimed he had nothing against marriage, indeed his own, though brief, had been unbelievably happy, but he preferred to think of himself as a loner. He'd said it, or thought it, in most of the premier cities of Europe, proving he had a generous coating of immunity to back up his words. Because scores of women, beautiful, talented, once even a titled lady, pursued him with a feminine relentlessness that made fiction of all the books she'd read, because wasn't man supposed to be the hunter?

Perhaps Angela had something on the others at that: patience. She hid her predatory instincts behind a facade of indifference, which intrigued him and made him want to penetrate it. Karen was not fooled, despite her youth she recognized it for the subtle ploy it was. And was forced to watch in silent anguish. Just because she wore a counterfeit smile, it didn't follow that her heart was made of cardboard.

'I don't want to share him,' she thought with childish irritation. A one child/one parent relationship is very possessive. She wasn't spoilt or in the least brattish, although she could have been excused these failings, but she was human. It's human to want to keep what is yours, and her father had belonged exclusively to her for a very long time.

But in the end it wasn't even a question of sharing, and this was the worst anguish of all. It hadn't occurred to her that a daughter almost as old as his love might be regarded as a liability. Until he intimated as much. Not brutally, of course, but word wrapped to sound as if it was for her own good.

'I've thought for a long time you should go home and learn some gentle, civilised ways.' Despite their years of voluntary exile they'd always thought of England as that. 'You're old enough to cast off on your own now. Be strong, be independent. Be my daughter.'

Which did her out of a good old-fashioned cry. His daughter would never indulge in foolish tears, but would stoically accept that a chapter of her life had come to a close. A chapter that had been made up of ecstasy and pain, joy and frustration. She would allow herself a wistful regret, favourably renaming the uneventful, boring moments, now calling them 'those beautiful, peaceful days' before turning to the new chapter with eagerness and gusto. That was the message her head relayed, there was only one thing wrong, no matter how hard she tried she couldn't rid herself of resentment, and her heart couldn't dredge up the smallest grain of comfort. How fervently she wished it was made of cardboard.

'You're not eating,' observed her table companion, nudging her back to the present.

'I'm not very hungry.'

His left eyebrow lifted. 'Not very talkative, either.'

'I know you mean it kindly,' she said. 'But you can't help me.'

He wouldn't be deflected. 'Sometimes it helps just to talk.'

His persistence didn't annoy her, or make her feel hot under the collar. She took a momentary pause to analyse her feelings; she knew she felt comfortable with him, but it was a shock to discover she felt partially ironed out just by being in his company. Yet he didn't look a soothing presence. Falling over that thought came another: a longing to unburden. Eventually she would have to unload to somebody, she couldn't keep it locked inside her for ever, so what better confidant than a stranger. Someone who wouldn't be around to remind her of her indiscretion.

She took another sip of wine, but even before the liquid had time to do more than pleasantly warm her throat, her tongue was tumbling out words, sounding inordinately pleased to do so.

CHAPTER TWO

A beginning, of sorts, found itself. To establish the bond between her father and self, she told him in a brief, few words of the mother with the soft voice and gentle hands, who occasionally stirred a tear in the memory bowl. It would have been nice (he thought she deliberately chose that placid little word, which conveyed only a shallow emotion) to have belonged to an ordinary family, with the usual quota of parents and perhaps a brother and sister thrown in. But such a wonderful, gay, charming, talented father (certainly an improvement on 'nice') outweighed any disadvantages.

She used her fingers to tick off his assets with a childlike exuberance that had an adverse effect. She would have been horrified to know he was silently thumbing in her beloved parent's failings. Irresponsibility came fairly high on the list, as she word-painted a spindling child in unisex clothes. Scrubbed shorts, faded cotton tee shirt, looking more boy than girl, slightly more trouble than a kitten, less of an encumbrance than a parcel that is made to tramp the earth at the whim of a tube of vermilion.

At intervals he interrupted to ask questions of a personal nature. Instead of the snub he merited, she answered each impertinence in a frank, unabashed fashion. She was twenty-one. That surprised him as he had set her a year or so under. Eventually she must get a job. No, she had neither particular talent, nor training of any sort. She had acted as her father's unpaid housekeeper, chauffeur, general runabout—you name it, she was it—and there hadn't been time to think about training for a career. Anyway she couldn't envisage the day she'd need to fend for herself.

Now that her hair had dried out he saw it was a rich, russet brown colour. A strand had escaped on to her cheek and was almost in her mouth. He picked it off and tucked it behind her ear. For no valid reason, except that he enjoyed man's normal appreciation of such things, he thought about her legs. He would like to have seen her in those unisex shorts.

This intriguing notion was uppermost in his

12

mind when she stopped talking, this time to stare, and not merely recharge her breath. The silence between them was unobtrusive, gentle, but her thoughts were busy. He tried to read them in her eyes, and in succeeding, choked.

'Drop of wine went down the wrong way,' he said, making that his excuse as it seemed unkind to laugh at her. She was so splendidly serious.

'I must ask,' she began.

'Please do,' he encouraged, if with marked reluctance.

'Although I find it dreadfully embarrassing.' —He found it dreadfully amusing—'But,'— she leaned forward, imperilling her glass— 'I've just had the most appalling thought. These things do happen. A girl can't be too careful. So, what I mean is, are you picking me up?'

The same hand that had lifted the hair off her cheek, an intimate gesture that had probably set her thoughts on their present course, reached out to steady her glass. 'No.' He matched her earnestness. 'I am not picking you up.' It seemed wise to add: 'I am showing a kindly interest.' His voice travelled on a razor edge as he thought she would prefer a cutting tone to one of ridicule.

Her eyes glinted. With joy? Disbelief? Her prosaic little nod told him nothing. 'That's all right then. I had to ask, though. You do see that, don't you?'

He wasn't altogether sure that he did, but he said: 'Yes.'

'That's all right then,' she repeated. 'Because I'm drinking your wine I don't want you to think . . .' She left the finish of the sentence to his imagination.

'Would you like a refill?' he enquired, adding a cautious, 'No strings attached.'

'You're laughing at me,' she reproved, a shoot of colour entering her cheeks. 'You're thinking, How dare this unpretentious, unpretty little madam suggest . . . well, you know.' She didn't enlarge, she didn't need to. He put her obsession down to either teasing promiscuity or total inexperience. He noticed, not without amusement, she called herself unpretty and not ordinary or plain. He agreed unpretty had a much nicer ring to it. If he hadn't been treading delicate ground he would have said, I like your modesty. I find it refreshing, different. But you're not unpretty, as you so charmingly put it. Your looks don't ravish, by that I mean they don't snatch a man's breath away but, and this is the nonplussing bit, take it just the same by less fair, more subtle means. But that would have sounded as if she was on the right track, so he said nothing.

She tapped the table, with a poke of aggression she said: 'Let me tell you, men think my type are easy game. They seem to think they are paying us a compliment!'

'Horrible creatures, men!' he quipped, trying to jolly the conversation into less dangerous channels.

Her eyelashes descended. He noticed they had golden tips, soft and feathery. When they lifted a thoughtful moment later, he saw that the eyes were forgiving. He thought it would be nice to know what miscalculation of thought or deed he was being forgiven. It was safer not to ask. Safer to say: 'Do you find England strange after so many years abroad?'

'Strange, disturbing, beautiful. Oh yes, despite the weather.' Her humour readily asserted itself. 'Perhaps because of the weather! The air feels so soft, and everything is so green. But,' her smile was displaced as she was swept with melancholy. 'There's always a but, isn't there? I didn't want to come like this. I didn't want it to be this way.' She looked down at her hands, clasped tightly together to almost endanger circulation.

'You know, I can't help thinking if I'd been younger things would have been different.'

'In what way could they have been different?'

'I don't know, really. Yes I do. I reminded them too much of the gap in their ages. If I'd been about eight they might not have noticed me.' Her voice took on a wistful note. 'I wish I could be eight again. I'd give everything I possess, including Darling Ugly, to be able to put the clock back.'

'Who, or what, is Darling Ugly?'

'My troll doll. And good luck mascot. He's so ugly, nobody could love him.'

'Except you.'

'Except me.' Her glance travelled to the bulge in the pocket of her coat, gently steaming near the radiator. 'He goes everywhere with me. My father gave him to me one birthday, oh ages ago, and I've treasured him ever since. I don't think he's brought me much luck. But I have the feeling that if I lost him, through carelessness, some dreadful disaster would befall me.'

Was he laughing at her? No, but he looked stern and displeased.

'It's a bad thing to be ruled by superstition,' he said. 'But I suppose your environment played some part of that.' For the first time he was in accord with her father. She hadn't come home a moment too soon.

'Have you ever wanted to put the clock back?' She pushed an agitated hand through her hair, but in fact she wanted to poke a way through his impregnable manner of cool assurance. His reply was perfectly in keeping and the one she expected.

'No, I can't say that I have.'

'But at some time or other you must have come up against a tough situation. One you couldn't bear to face.'

'Yes.' His mouth and his eyes and even the angle of his chin, rebuked.

'But putting the clock back wouldn't solve anything. It would only put off,'—he deliberately refrained from saying, the evil moment, and said instead, 'The situation you thought you couldn't bear to face. Eventually you would have to shoulder up to it.'

'Yes, yes I see. You're saying that some day I would have to let go of my father's hand. And better today than tomorrow.' This one should be up in a pulpit, yes even with those fiendish eyes, she thought. Her smile had been trembling near the surface for the past few seconds, now it trampled the barrier of good old honest indignation and the sudden, delightful lift of her mouth exploded the myth of plainness once and for all.

'Thank you. You've been a regular,'—she hoped she didn't sound too sarcastic—'what's the word?'

'Samaritan?'

'Yes, samaritan. Now, how many pesetas worth of food do you think I've eaten?'

'None,' he said drily. 'Haven't you any English money?'

'Of course. I might be confused. But I'm not insolvent!' Blast the man. He was laughing at her again. And did he always have to put her in the wrong!

He reminded himself that she wasn't his responsibility, but right away asked:

'What are your plans? I assume you have something mapped out?'

17

'Oh yes. Right now I intend to take myself off to the station to board a train to Weighbridge.'

He didn't usually double his mistakes and assuredly it was a mistake to ask: 'What's at Weighbridge?'

'A bridge, I should think.' Her eyes brightened suspiciously. 'You know, if Dad hadn't met Angela, he'd probably be sitting here with us now. We'd planned to come to England on a motoring holiday. Well, just because there's only me, I don't see why I should ditch the original plan. My father was very generous.' She leaned forward, pathetically eager to show her parent in the best possible light. 'He insisted on giving me all his savings, so that I could invest in a small car and see a bit of the country and still have enough to tide me over until I get a job.' With touching dignity she took out her wallet to pay her bill.

Dare he offer to pay it for her? Certainly he had been well entertained. But no, his generous impulse was certain to be misread. She would undoubtedly accuse him of trying to buy her for the night.

Which one, which one? Teasing promiscuity or total inexperience. It was as well that after today he would not have to see her again. He had complications enough.

'Goodbye.' She juggled with the conglomeration of suitcase, tartan holdall and

18

cream leather handbag, so that she could put out her hand. It was slim and brown, with unvarnished, almond shaped nails. He felt reluctant to take it. He frowned as a wave of annoyance swept over him. Yet he couldn't allow himself to get involved.

All the same. 'I can see you to the station,' he said, ungraciously relieving her of holdall and suitcase.

Outside, the rain had stopped, leaving the air sweet and soft. His long strides gobbled up the deep purple satin sash of road, as if, she thought, doubling her step to keep pace with him, he was anxious to be rid of her. Well, at least he was in fashion, she thought irritably.

'Goodbye,' she said for the second time, this time at the station entrance; but he brushed her hand aside, saying he might as well buy a platform ticket and see her on the train. Seeing the job through to its conclusion, she supposed with irrational bitterness.

The train was in. The third, and final, goodbye would be brief.

'I don't know your name,' he said.

'Nor I, yours.'

'It's Ian . . . Ian Nicholson. Here's my card. If ever you find yourself in serious straits, you must contact me.'

'I will,' she promised accepting the square of pasteboard. 'Oh, and I'm Karen Shaw.'

'Karen.' Quickly, quickly, because time was short, he rolled the name over his tongue. 'It suits you.'

A whistle blew. It struck a piercing, imperious note. Doors slammed, people hastened, somewhere a child cried. Voices were of necessity raised to a clamour, which receded, to return with the gathered impetus of a sonic boom, spreading its audible strength to the far reaches of the darkening streets beyond.

'Well Karen, this is it.'

'Yes, this is it.' Her voice was stiff with urgency. This is it. The sand had run out. There was no more time left for him to infuriate her, amuse, chide and comfort her. Three cheers. Who wanted this smug, arrogant fiend-man with the devil-grin lurking to eat up his super serious mouth. Gosh, he was a bigger challenge than the world of loneliness and uncertainty that faced her. She could handle it; whatever came she must handle it with chin up at the ready. Strong, fearless she was. No problem, surely. Except . . . why did she feel so strange, so shattered? It wasn't like her at all.

Her mind turned slowly, meditatively. How could she know what she was like? Truly like? It had been easy to be strong and fearless and quietly resolute with her father's hand slung carelessly round her shoulders; easy to be brave when faced with a chest massive enough to burrow her head against, her cheek at a tilt to receive his smacking kiss. Her father was an undemonstrative man who always curtailed his emotions, and yet it was her cherished belief he enjoyed those spontaneous bursts of affection as much as she did. Would he miss the loving soft snuggle? No, because now he had Angela, his Angel as he called her, to satisfy such needs. She wasn't quite his Angel yet, but she soon would be. Now that he had cast off the appendage of a daughter, he would feel free to woo the lady.

An appendage . . . a parasitic creature who had to be told it was time to stop hanging on. The hurt of it pricked her eyes and it was suddenly necessary to tug a frantic hand in her pocket for her handkerchief. As the square of lace trimmed cotton travelled speedily upwards, something soft brushed against her legs. She was going to bend down to investigate, when two hands made light captive of her shoulders, and a mouth touched hers.

The unexpectedness of it relieved her of coherent thought. Yet even she knew platform kisses were stock. All about them goodbye kisses were given and taken, some prolonged and passionate, others as light as the parting token she had just received.

They broke away and he bundled her on the gently moving train. Well, now he knew. Not teasing promiscuity at all. She'd been riding him, challenging him, out of curiosity. Inexperience can be very curious, he thought, dimly remembering his own green youth.

Something disturbed him. Not her actions,

21

it wasn't the first time a girl had blatantly invited a kiss, the twist, the thought to munch on was his mishandling of the situation. He didn't know how, or why, but that kiss had been a liberty. His blandness, the quality of assurance she had secretly admired in him, gave way to an inability to reason properly. Because, heck! what's a kiss in this contemporary age? Not even a kiss, but an innocent peck. So why did he feel guilt-ridden?

His thoughts checked right there, because it wasn't only guilt he felt as he viewed the rear end of the fast receding train, but something else. Sharp, with a zealous kick. In a word: dismay.

CHAPTER THREE

The heavy carriage door slammed shut. From its slow start the train surged forward like an animal in pursuit of the night, which now wasn't so very far ahead. Already the gloom of evening was pressing against the windows and the line of cottages, running parallel with the track, flowered, one by one, into light.

Karen viewed the gathering dusk with feelings of disquiet. It would be dark by the time the train pulled into Weighbridge. She began to wish she'd stayed put, the prospect of looking for overnight accommodation was a gloomy one and she could well do without this hindrance. She tried to estimate the actual time of arrival, but his face kept getting in the way. A tender tyrant with chameleon eyes: kind for a second, satanic and condemning the other fifty-nine. Odd to think they would never meet again. Yet if there had been a possibility of a future encounter she would never have unburdened in that juvenile fashion. It seemed incredible that she had. Normally she was a reticent sort of person, but these weren't normal circumstances.

Life used to be so placid. She could remember back to a time when she'd sighed for something out of the ordinary to happen. Nothing dramatic or spectacular, but something to enliven the set pattern of her life.

Perhaps she'd brought misfortune upon herself by being dissatisfied with her lot. The beginning hadn't been Angela, as she had led Ian to believe; the real beginning had been the night of the storm. Fate had pointed its finger and said, 'Let's teach this Miss a lesson.' It was one she could not forget, yet found too painful to remember.

She deliberately turned her thoughts away, seeking a distraction that was pleasant and amusing. That platform kiss had been pleasant and amusing—now she was happily diverted—and instructional and enjoyable. Had he enjoyed it? She was inclined to think he had. He might have considered her a bit of a nuisance, but that hadn't stopped him finding her kissable. At the actual moment of kissing, her eyes had been closed, so she didn't know what his face had registered; but afterwards a telling tenderness had driven away his justifiable irritation. Poor man, he hadn't known what he was letting himself in for when he first struck up a conversation. That would teach him not to let sympathy override common sense!

Well, anyway, it was nice to know she hadn't lost her sense of humour. But a sense of humour makes a frail blanket for a cold and weary traveller. She had been up since long before dawn and the hours prior to that had been robbed of sleep by excitement and apprehension. She reached in her pocket for her good luck mascot, her bit of comfort, but all her fingers met was the silk of her pocket lining. Darling Ugly wasn't there. Then she knew what had brushed her legs in falling on to the station platform. She must have pulled the troll doll out with her handkerchief.

The hotel she finally decided upon, after a brisk walk down dismal, inadequately lit streets, was red bricked, totally unimpressive. The inside was as unadorned and as depressing as the exterior, but at least it was clean. A dour little man with greying hair, after informing her firmly that the restaurant was closed for the night and she couldn't hope for a hot meal, showed her to her room.

She had to bite her lip to stop herself from apologizing too profusely for being such a great trouble. After all, it was a hotel. Then she thought, well, perhaps it's his rheumatism, he walked with a rheumaticky gait, and as he swung open the unprepossessing brown door she flashed him a hoydenish smile. His mouth parted in a toothy grin, which might or might not have been in response to her smile. More likely it was due to the generous tip she pressed into his hand.

Brown paintwork, fawn linoleum, a top-heavy wardrobe that was old old, not antique. But her eye barely registered the room; all she could see was the bed. High, she almost needed a step-stool to climb in, and then it was like floating on goosefeathers. It was so soft and warm and she was asleep.

Next morning she ducked out of bacon and eggs and breakfasted on toast and marmalade. During her years of exile she had eaten lightly for this first meal of the day, following the continental custom, and she hadn't sufficient faith in the hotel to wish to renew old taste habits. After breakfast she checked out and went in search of a garage showroom.

The little car, which just had to be her little car, was parked temptingly in the forecourt with a price ticket affixed to its windscreen. It was red and she could just see herself behind the wheel, the window wound right down so that the wind would ruffle her hair as she bowled along the open road.

Carefully she pocketed the necessary documents, M.O.T. certificate and the insurance cover note. After much deliberation she had decided to risk it and insure third party as the difference between that and full comprehensive cover would bed and breakfast her for a few nights. And she wasn't going to have an accident. She never had and she'd been driving since she was seventeen.

And yet, because of the unfamiliar driving conditions, at first she gritted her teeth and pressed her foot very lightly down on the accelerator. How green everything looked. Green, green, incredibly green. It seemed to her she had never seen so many variations of this wonderful colour. As she negotiated her first traffic-free country road, she relaxed her grim determination and delighted in so much lush vegetation and velvety greenness. After living in a country where so-called green has a yellowish tint, vegetation is sparse, and each brave blade of grass is frizzled by the fierce heat of the sun, it was as if her starved eyes couldn't get their fill. And yet she allowed herself only quick sideways glances, which, as things turned out, probably saved her life.

The road had more curves than a camel's back; rounding the second successive hump she was confronted by a yellow car, travelling at a fantastic speed. On the wrong side of the road!

Instinctively she wrenched at the wheel. The car careered across the grass verge; the moment its tail-end was no longer imperilled by the yellow car, she jumped on the brake, but her timing was a split second too late. The vehicle was already shuddering on a precipitous bank, and to her horror it fell away into nothing. It was the most numbing moment of her life. Her hands were ineffectually gripping the steering wheel, when it came to her with sickening clarity, that in a situation such as this, driving skill counted for nothing. Her fate was, literally, in other, more blessedly competent hands; all she could do was ignore the drumming noise in her ears and pray to remain fully conscious. She mustn't allow herself the sweetness of oblivion, not yet.

But, oh! the temptation to let the horrible reality slip away and feel soft, black nothing. She felt so drowsy. If only that hysterical female would stop screaming. Then she realized she was alone in the car and the anguished sound was coming from her own throat. Perhaps she was shocked into awareness, because now she was alert to her plight. She rolled herself into a ball and protected her head with her hands. She remembered reading somewhere that it was important to protect the head. In the event she was ready, and reasonably prepared for the final dull thud as the car's two front wheels slid neatly and inexorably into the ditch.

Now that it was over, now that the skyline had stopped chasing the bank, and the car was holding more or less steady, she marvelled that so much agony could be crammed into a few seconds.

Then she realized it wasn't over, not with so much petrol splashed around. The smell of it hit her stomach and as she clawed at the door she didn't know how she managed not to be sick. The door lever went down all right, but the door wouldn't open. It was jammed. Now, she was not only fighting nausea, but fear. It wasn't the first time she had known real fear. She thought it unjust, cruel even, that some people are allowed to go through life without incident, whereas she had faced death twice.

Well, she had escaped it once, if not unscathed, so why not again? Perhaps her worst fear wouldn't be justified. The petrol tank didn't have to explode.

She renewed her efforts to get out, putting her shoulder to the door and heaving with all her might. Nothing happened. She gritted her teeth and tried again, perhaps desperation lent strength because this time the door gave and she half fell into the foul-smelling ditch. Except that as she fell, stumbled, crawled, two or three steps, it was the sweetest smell in the world.

A shadow fell over her and a voice, it was male and very angry, demanded: 'What the hell were you trying to do? Kill yourself? And me, too? You little fool, don't you know better than to—'

He must be the driver of the yellow car. She hadn't thought about it, but it was reasonable to assume he would come to her aid. Especially as he had driven her into the ditch. That unspeakably horrid ditch. She was aware now of the slime and the smell and she didn't know whether to cry or belt into him. He hadn't even had the common decency to ask her if she was hurt. Was she hurt? Well, her dignity had taken a trouncing and her shoulder throbbed painfully, and if that wasn't enough she must look an absolute sight. And it was all his fault!

She screamed: 'You maniac driver! You're an imbecile, a menace to all road users. You're a—' She wished he would keep still. She couldn't see his face properly. Looking at him was like looking at a distorted film.

'I'm sorry,' she stammered. 'I think—'

'It's all right. I was angry with you because you gave me a fright. Relax, now, I'll take care of you.' Something was wrong with his voice. It was coming to her through wads of cotton wool. She thought he was lifting her. The ground certainly went from beneath her feet. She protested, saying that if he'd give her a minute or two to collect herself, she'd be able to walk. Something—smoke or fumes?—was stinging her eyes and choking her throat, making it difficult to breathe, let alone speak.

She felt his arm tighten round her body as they began to climb, presumably out of the ditch. It was all very hazy. He didn't seem to be taking any notice of her protests; instead he told her to stop wriggling. She must have obeyed because progress suddenly became easier. Her throat stopped feeling as if it had been scrubbed raw, and she began to experience a delicious sensation, like swimming under water. The crystal water round her island home had been perfect for aqua sports. How she had loved poking about among the rocks, identifying the different species of brightly coloured fish: red, coral, darts of pure dazzling gold. Oh! such pretty colours danced before her eyes! But what was that terrific noise? Eruption? Explosion? Now she was falling through layers of soft midnight blue . . . down . . . down . . . down.

She knew she was in hospital. In a spotlessly clean bed. Who could have put her in such a beautifully clean bed, when she was covered from head to toe in mud and slime? But she was no longer dirty, even her hair felt silky and clean. The man in the yellow car had gone away and another man stood in his place. A doctor in a white coat. In a little while he, too, went away, but she was not alone. Her tender tyrant sat by her bed, holding her hand.

She felt comforted and at peace. She didn't think it strange for him to be there. It felt natural and right. 'Hello,' she said. 'You do get

30

around.'

'Come to think of it,' he said, his voice stern and grave, just the way it had sounded in the restaurant, 'the same might be said of you.'

She pouted. 'If you're going to be cross and disapproving, I shall go to sleep.'

He said drily: 'You will, anyway. You've been given something to make you rest.'

'Is that why I feel whooshy?' She giggled. 'The last time I felt like this was when I drank three glasses of Sangria straight off. That's a local drink, you know, and very potent.'

'I've heard of it,' he said. 'There's one vital difference. When you wake in the morning you won't have a hangover or any nasty after-effects. Which is a darned sight more than you deserve.' After that she did go to sleep.

It was morning when she awoke and the events of yesterday had taken on the elusive quality of a dream, or a sunbeam that for ever dances out of reach. She wasn't surprised to find herself in hospital, she remembered that much. It was the events leading up to her admission that were hazy.

She was in a private ward with green emulsioned walls. She thought green was a very tranquil colour. She wasn't very keen on the hospital smell of carbolic soap and strong antiseptic.

A nurse came in. When she touched her forehead, her hand felt as deliciously cold as marble and her voice was as soft as an angel's—she had been thinking in terms of an angel's wing, but for some reason that seemed to evade her, she had an aversion to angels—so she substituted, as soft as a kitten's paw in play.

'Come, rouse yourself, Miss Shaw. You've had your beauty sleep.'

'Why am I here?'

'In the cottage hospital?'

A thermometer was popped into her mouth. She pushed it out with her tongue.

'What am I doing in hospital? I'm not poorly.'

The nurse retrieved the thermometer and the kitten's paw opened to reveal a tiger's sharp claw. 'No, not poorly, or you would have been in the infirmary. Now, we will endeavour to take your temperature. And no nonsense this time, if you please!'

It seemed politic not to argue with the tiger's claw.

'Good, very good,' beamed nurse. 'Normal. Your brother will be pleased.'

Karen thought it as well to point out the error. 'I haven't got a brother,' she said, thinking magnanimously that it was a wonder mistakes of this sort weren't made more often. Poor thing, if she was icily impatient and harassed, it was probably because she was rushed off her feet. A moment later, as the nurse rounded on her, she felt her sympathy was misplaced.

'Really!' clicked the sharp tongue. 'You are very trying this morning.'

'I haven't got a brother,' repeated Karen firmly.

'No? And I haven't got a difficult patient! Now, stop! Otherwise I won't let him visit.'

'When?'

'Now.'

Karen sat up in bed, her eyes were round and incredulous. 'Perhaps I do have a brother. Perhaps I'm poorly and don't know it. I might be concussed.'

Tetchily nurse said: 'Yes,' trying hard to anchor her patience. 'Perhaps that's it.'

But Karen meant it. She thought it cruel of the nurse to resort to satire when she felt helpless and confused. Yet she didn't know why this should be so because her head felt beautifully clear. Just as Ian had predicted. Had he really visited her yesterday evening? Sat by her bed, held her hand?

She was remembering everything now: buying the car, crashing it. Her thoughts went back to the evening prior to the accident, and a tide of crimson washed her cheeks. In the restaurant she had only been able to pour out her heart to him, because he wasn't a permanency in her life. She would never have confided those intimate details if there had been the slightest possibility of meeting up with him again. She must hurry and discharge herself from hospital, in case he decided to pay a second visit. As soon as this ridiculous brother business was cleared up, she would put it to nurse.

On the heels of this thought, came nurse, this time not alone.

'Here is your brother,' she said, gushing sweetness, obviously for his sake.

'Oh brother!' croaked Karen.

'Sister dear,' said Ian, bending to peck her cheek. 'You gave me quite a fright.' His tone was indulgent, kindly even, but his eyes were as fiendishly condemning as ever. She thought she must have been at a very low ebb to think of him as a tender tyrant. Just plain tyrant was nearer the mark.

'I should have known it was you,' she said in a hoarse whisper. 'Why do you say you're my brother?'

'M—m.' He tugged at his chin and pretended to study her face with deep—and brotherly?—concern. 'You are in a mood, aren't you?' he had the audacity to say, and then, to Karen's choking indignation, he turned to nurse and blandly volunteered: 'My sister can be very tiresome at times. Her arrival was,'—the beast, he had the gall to grin openly at Karen—'to say the least, unexpected. I'm afraid we've all contributed to spoiling her. You know how it is?'

'Indeed I do,' sympathised nurse, continuing to look at him in a foolish, besotted way. Apparently some behind the scene calefaction had taken place; somehow he had managed to defrost Miss Frozen Tiger's Paw and had bamboozled her into believing his lie. Nothing Karen could say would convince her Ian hadn't spoken the truth.

'And now,' said nurse. 'I'll leave you. You must have lots to discuss.'

Indeed yes, thought Karen, and was further mortified by nurse's parting shot. 'Now behave yourself, Miss. Your conduct has been irresponsible, foolhardy and totally lacking in consideration for others. If I were your brother I should be sorely tempted to take you across my knee and spank some sense into you.'

'We-ll!' gasped Karen. Rounding on Ian she commanded: 'Call her back. Tell her she can't speak to me like that.'

'But she already has,' he pointed out with exasperating truth. 'And what sound advice. I'm almost tempted.'

'I th-think you're h-horrible,' she said, anger thrusting a stammer in her voice. 'A . . . a tyrant!'

'That's the thanks I get for coming all this way.'

She remembered. 'That's another thing. Why did you? Or should that be how did you? How on earth did you manage to find me?'

'I didn't,' he explained. 'The hospital authorities found me. The card I gave you at the railway station was in your pocket. Muddy but readable. You had no other identification on you.'

'I see.' A thought struck her and she amended that to: 'No, I don't see. Why did you say you were my brother?'

'I said stepbrother. To cover the discrepancy in our names.'

'But why?' She tried to sound detached and not jellied by his severe countenance.

He conceded: 'I suppose I could have said we were engaged. But I don't affiance myself to children. If you mean, why did I claim relationship, the answer is simple. It was the only way to get you discharged in my care.' For the first time she noticed the green and gold carrier bag in his hands. He was clutching it— nervously? Or was that too fanciful a notion. She couldn't imagine anything putting him out. He was saying: 'Look, I'm not an ogre.' Not ogre, tyrant. 'I couldn't let you roam the streets. And I couldn't be sure you'd enough sense to contact your father. So it seemed the only solution. Don't you agree?'

'Only to disagree,' she said tightly.

He chided: 'I think you're being stubborn and ridiculous. Stop acting like a child and get dressed. Then we can get out of this place. Or have you developed an attachment for the hospital? I almost said nurse, but thought your sense of humour might not have that much stretch. Ah! you're smiling. I was beginning to think you'd forgotten how.'

'I'm beginning to see I don't have a choice.'

36

'Good girl.' As he spoke he tipped the carrier bag—he was nervous she realized in mute fascination—clumsily on the bed, and out billowed a dress in a stunning shade of emerald. 'How clever of you,' he said, his smile bashful, his cheeks glowing brick red, 'to have eyes the exact colour of this dress. I hope the . . . ehm . . . fit is right.' He gave the carrier bag another shake and out fell a dainty underneath set with a lace trim and microscopic pink roses, and a bra with the size ticket and name of a well known store still attached.

She stared dumbly at his suddenly averted profile. 'Yes, but these aren't my clothes. I want my clothes.' Her voice took on a shrill note and she knew that if he took her to task for acting like a child again, it would be a just criticism. It was because she was afraid, afraid to explore that one dark corner of her mind. Like a child she was cringing from the unknown, probably imagined, terror. That was it. It was her imagination. How often had her father said, 'One day that imagination of yours is going to knock you for six.' There was no terror, no unprobed corner, and yet . . .

'Don't torture yourself,' he said with kindly insight. 'Concentrate on getting through today. Tomorrow is soon enough to talk.'

'There's something to talk about?'

'Nothing serious. Will you take my word for that? I can't have you fretting unnecessarily.' But as he stopped measuring the tip of his shoe to slant her a sideways glance, he saw she was fretting. It had to be discussed now.

'What do you remember?' He folded his hands and flung the question at her nonchalantly.

'Crashing the car.'

'Anything else?'

'Yes. The reason I crashed.' She paused to draw a needful breath. 'It was an unfamiliar make of car and that being so I was handling it with excessive caution. The road was twisty, so I didn't see the yellow car until it was almost on top of me. That idiot driver! He came hell for leather round the bend, on my side of the road! If I hadn't swerved into the ditch it would have been a head-on collision.'

'I think it is only fair to point out,' he inserted tonelessly, 'that the idiot driver, as you call him, acted with commendable presence of mind and saved you from possible burns.' He was watching her closely, as if he'd given her the vital piece of a jigsaw puzzle, and it was only a matter of moments before she clicked it into place and made complete a hitherto senseless picture.

'Yes, I remember bits. I was semi-conscious when he reached me. I think I was pretty far gone because I'd concentrated all my efforts on getting out of that wretched car. I did get out, didn't I? Under my own steam, I mean? The door was jammed but I thought—?'

'Yes,' he said in that same, unemotional

monotone. 'You got out. Howard Mitchell, that's the name of your rescuer arrived in time to carry you clear.'

'I'm sorry, but from that point I only seem to remember colours. Fiery, flashing colours in shades of red, orange and yellow. I don't know why. But wait a minute, I believe I do know why. You said he saved me from possible burns. That can only mean—' She covered her face with her hands as partial realization washed over her. (The immensity of her loss didn't hit her until later). She didn't want him to see the torment in her eyes.

'I think I knew all along,' she said at last. 'Deep down I knew the petrol tank had exploded. The car is—?'

'A write-off.'

'Oh!' she gulped.

'What is it?' His eyes seemed to burn a way through her fingers, yet, surprisingly, his tone was uncritical and she knew she had not earned his contempt. 'Didn't you insure?'

'Only third party. Foolish of me. Not only am I accident prone, but I do foolish things, take ridiculous chances. Was nothing saved?'—hopefully.

'No.'

'My suitcase, my handbag containing every penny I owned was in that car.' Even then it was doubtful if it fully registered. He took hold of her fingers and lifted them away from her face.

'Look at me!' His voice was a thrust, a roar, a command. 'You can look at me. Feel me.' As his voice, by its strength and enthusiasm, impelled her to hear, his fingers folded round hers, forcing her to know, and acknowledge, the sensation of touch. 'You can feel me with your own two good hands. You can get out of that bed and walk out of this hospital on your own two good legs. Isn't that wonderful? Marvellous? Aren't you the luckiest girl alive!' He paused, shaken. As if the wonder and magnanimity had only just penetrated. Gruffly, how gruffly, how humbly he said:

'You're alive, Karen. Within a week the scratch on your arm will disappear, the bruise on your cheek, fade. You're a whole woman.'

A whole woman . . . lucky to be alive . . . breathing, feeling, seeing.

Why couldn't she gloat? Where was the glorious feeling of exultation?

Her hand found the hollow at the base of her throat. This time her face might have been marked. That would have been more shattering than . . .

But everything. Possessions are nothing, until you haven't got any to possess. Her fingers danced away from his, to curl into mallets and hammer the pillow. 'That idiot! That damned idiot! If only he'd been looking where he was going.'

Ian's mouth twisted with a hint of wryness. 'Before you start apportioning the blame,

40

how's your driving?'

Her eyes blazed green fire. 'I drove for my father. Let me tell you I've driven on some of the best roads in Europe!'

'That may be,' he said quietly. 'But this is England. The land of quaint customs. One of them happens to be driving on the left side of the road.' He nudged the emerald green dress with superior largess. 'Put this on.' In other words, wrap up, forget it. But she couldn't.

'You mean—?' Her voice was a croak, a plea; she retreated from arrogance and self-righteous indignation and fell back on a pair of haunted eyes. 'It was my fault?' Oh, dear God, no! Not that, not that.

But his continued silence told her it was, indeed, the truth. The man in the yellow car was blameless. She was the one guilty of driving on the wrong side of the road.

CHAPTER FOUR

Her thoughts were strewn haphazardly. She began collecting them up. She had set off driving on the left side of the road, but she must have grown careless . . .

She didn't want to go with him, his high-handedness was virtually kidnap, but in her present state of weakness, she hadn't the will to resist.

. . . The mind does grow careless when the eye is enchanted.

The dress was a perfect fit. The addition of a bra (Had he really walked into a store, selected and paid for it?) improved her figure. She had got into the relaxed habit of not wearing one. Her own sandals, well scrubbed, were located in the bedside locker. Nothing else, apparently, had been salvaged. He'd forgotten to purchase stockings; not that it mattered, her legs were the colour stocking manufacturers had been trying to create for years.

With quiet fuss, goodbyes all round, he escorted her out to his car. It was a shadow-grey saloon. Infnitely superior to the one she'd 'bent'.

He opened the door for her with polite solicitude. 'Well?' he questioned, when she hesitated.

Surely it's the easiest thing in the world to get in a car. There are two ways. You sit in, and swing your legs in after you. Or you duck your head and walk in. Not quite as elegant as the first way, but as effective. But she could neither sit in, nor walk in, nor even explain. Her feet had suddenly acquired ton weights, and her tongue was locked solid.

He tapped his foot in a gesture of impatience. 'Well? What are you waiting for?' His shrewd glance, not damning, but not sympathetic either, summed up the situation.

'Oh, I see! After-crash symptoms,' he diagnosed. 'Well, it so happens I know the remedy for that.'

She felt her elbow taken hold of, and her feet left the ground. It was a dream with rose petal edges; only her relief was real, because he wasn't going to make her get in that dreaded passenger seat. But the rose petals faded, to disintegrate into black ash; and the dream turned into a nightmarish reality as she realized exactly what he did intend.

'I . . . ca-can't. Even you couldn't be cruel enough to make me drive.' Her plea was as ineffective as a leaf tapping against the weathered bark of a tree.

His reply was sharp and woody. 'Yes, I can be that cruel.'

Her brow felt clammy and her jaw was slack with self pity.

'Oh, brace up, girl!' he ordered, sounding so reasonably exasperated that her limbs automatically reacted and folded into the driving seat. Having installed himself in the passenger seat, he reached over and switched on the ignition.

'Come on, foot on the clutch and into first gear.' He sounded like a scornful driving instructor urging a not very bright pupil. She thought, I don't think I've ever hated anyone quite so intensely ever before, and her jaw firmed as her hands tightened on the wheel. 'Which way?'

At first it was like driving all the way to Hell, but after a while her back lost its rigidity and she found, if not complete enjoyment in a relaxation that had, in the past, given her many hours of pure pleasure, at least a measure of confidence.

'There,' he said, from his slouched down position, almost as if he had a periscopic view of her mind. 'Not so very bad, is it?'

Her breath lumped in her throat and she said testily: 'I hope you know I have just relived the second worst moment of my life.'

He wondered what the worst moment was, but said: 'The accident? Well, I hoped you would have. You have to relive something in order to conquer it. If I'd said, "There, there, forget the nasty hurt," you might never have found the courage to drive again. Which would have been a pity. You are a competent driver.'

She was stung to retort: 'Please keep your compliments.'

With lazy deliberation he said: 'In all truth a compliment wasn't intended. I merely stated a truth. Now, take the first left and pull in at Sharpe's. It's a restaurant that serves rather good lunches. And I happen to be starving.'

But for all that he ordered spartanly for himself, though he gave her a free choice. She couldn't help but wonder if it wasn't his way of curtailing a first time after the event, ordeal.

She relished her pork chop with good appetite, and ordered, to follow, a sweet consisting of meringue, fresh cream and icecream, with just a sprinkling of chopped nuts. Then coffee. Although she had been firmly convinced she wouldn't be able to swallow a thing.

He left her drinking her coffee and went to make a telephone call. A business call. Had he neglected his work to drive out to fetch her? And why? Surely, when contacted, all he had to say was, 'I'm only a passing acquaintance.' There had been no reason for him to get involved.

She glanced out of the window. A car was pulling into the forecourt. A yellow car. She mustn't let the sight of a yellow car upset her. There must be hundreds of yellow cars on the roads, and she would be in a fine state if she jumped whenever she saw one.

But it was no good. Her mind had already jerked back and she was half way to Hell again. She was driving along the road and there seemed no way of avoiding collision with the yellow car; yet a tiny part of her mind rose above the agony, so that she could wonder what Ian would prescribe. A dozen yellow cars? Five hundred? A million?

She crammed her fists to her mouth and gradually the hysteria receded, so that she was calmed when the car's owner entered the dining room.

She watched his entry with a detached eye. Ian was taking a long time over his phone call, and she was beginning to feel restless. Studying the new arrival was something to do. He was tall, though not as tall as Ian, and stiffer built. He would never order a spartan meal. Fair hair, nose slightly aquiline, blue eyes fringed with excessively long and really dark lashes. Why did Nature favour men in this unfair way? Very fair complexion, with a peppering of fine laughter lines, as if he found life good sport and worth any effort. He sauntered, rather than walked, with a nerveless elegance; always completely at ease, he would prefer feminine to masculine company. This summing up, oddly enough, made him no less male. A very fine specimen, concluded Karen as he drew abreast with her table.

Instead of passing by, he stopped and greeted: 'So we meet again. This time in happier circumstances.'

Her hands gripped the edge of the tablecloth. 'Are you . . . you . . . the . . . ?'

'Idiot driving the other car?' His brow lifted in gentle amusement. 'Yes, you were semi-conscious when I reached you. I'm also a maniac driver, not fit to be let loose on a decent road. Shall I go on?'

'No.'

'Pity. The rest has a decidedly salty flavour. But this time I'll be gallant and spare your blushes. The name is Howard Mitchell. Call me Mitch. May I join you for a moment?'

'Yes, of course. Karen Shaw. I'm sorry for

not thinking, please do. My escort is making a telephone call.'

'Yes, Karen. I spotted friend Ian in the telephone booth when I passed. I may call you Karen? After what we've been through I can hardly call you Miss Shaw!'

'Not very well. In any case, I prefer Christian names. I hate formality. So, you and Ian are acquainted?'

'Ah . . . yes: We're not exactly on kissing terms. Tell me, how did a nice girl like you get in his clutches?'

She sighed. 'It's a long story. If ever you've an evening to spare, I'll tell you.'

'The day after tomorrow?' he suggested. 'That's Wednesday. Eightish? Here?'

'Oh, but I didn't mean . . . I wasn't angling.'

'I know, I know. But I am. I want to see you again. Is it on?'

'Well, I'm not sure of my plans.'

'But you'll try to make it?' Blue eyes have a knack of pressing sincerity.

'Yes, I'll try.' She felt breathless, out of her depth, grateful. This man had saved her from severe disability, or worse. He might even have saved her life, so that did partially obligate her. It also reminded her: 'I think thanks are in order. I believe you risked scorching your nose to drag me clear.'

'It was nothing,' he said. His grin spread like warmed treacle, and was every bit as sweet. 'I'd do the same for any winsome girl.' Then he leaned forward and pretended to screw a finger into the dimple to the left of her mouth, the dimple his sauciness had conjured up.

She saw Ian threading his way back to their table, and spotted the reaction on his face when he saw she was chatting to Mitch. Mitch hadn't lied when he said they weren't on kissing terms; they weren't on any terms as far as she could see, save, perhaps, bad ones. Ian's mouth clamped rigid, and it drew from her an involuntary: 'Oh dear! Here comes Big Brother!' But as he came nearer she wondered if she'd imagined the antagonism, because his face now wore the look of basic politeness one adopts when approaching someone who merely skirts the outer circle of one's acquaintance.

'Blast!' said Mitch. Then in undertones: 'Look, about Wednesday. Do try.'

'Yes, yes. I said I would. But don't wait too long for me if I can't make it.'

'No, I won't wait too long. Only for ever.' His voice was so faint it was little more than a breath curving down from her ear to her cheek, and her hand went up in a stupid way, as if words could be cupped, and kept.

Meanwhile, Mitch was raising his voice and saying with false heartiness:

'Hello, Ian, old chap! How's tricks? Haven't seen you at the club for weeks.'

'Golf,' said Ian for Karen's benefit, keeping his glance centred on Mitch. 'We are both fond of a round of golf. I've often thought that for two such opposite types, we share a marked similarity of taste.'

Whatever the thrust, it went home. Mitch looked slaughtered, and his cheeks paled to sheet-white.

'Ian and I were at school together,' he gabbled hastily, as if it was imperative to explain. 'In the same form.'

'And admired the same form,' came the swift reply. The nearest thing Karen could liken his tone to was crisp irony. She knew what it was like to be at the whipping end of Ian's tongue, and her heart went out to Mitch, looking so strained and white and funny. And the silence was even worse, because even though Ian stopped mincing him up with his tongue, his eyes went right on sharpening themselves on Mitch's by this time, averted profile.

She felt a desperate need to powder her nose, but she daren't for the life of her leave them alone. Bad as it was, she felt that while ever she remained at least they wouldn't come to blows.

'Shall we push off?' said Ian after what seemed like hours, but couldn't have been more than a hand-count of seconds.

'Yes.' Was that tight little voice hers? Oh dear, she hadn't meant to sound so condemning, even if she was. Mitch just didn't seem to be defending himself and she attributed this to a sweet and touching consideration for her.

She held out her hand. 'Goodbye, Mitch.' She smiled somewhat frantically, trying to convey her allegiance without using words. She thought, as their fingers touched in brief handclasp, he looked comforted, reassured that she hadn't gone over to the other side. Whether the exchange of glances was intercepted or not, her wrist was rudely clasped and she was speedily propelled from the dining room.

'What did you talk about?' demanded her abductor, his eyes dark and dictatorial.

'N . . . nothing,' she said, ashamed of the tremor in her voice. 'I thanked him for his presence of mind in dragging me clear of the wreckage.' She thought, what am I doing, apologising? I owe this man nothing! Well, perhaps a few clothes, and a hospital bill. Presumably he had paid. Certainly no one had presented her with a bill. All right, so she did owe him something, but it wasn't in her to grovel. Even though her heart was beating fast and she had been feeling decidedly queer for the past few minutes, she couldn't stop the arrogant lift of her chin as she inquired spiritedly: 'I trust thanks were in order.'

'Perfectly. You did the right thing. Now there is no need for you to talk to him again.'

'But he might talk to me first. Then what do I do?'

'I don't know. You're a woman. It's a woman's situation. Handle it. By the way, it's through there.'

'What is?'

'The ladies' room. If you want to powder your nose, I'll wait for you in the car.'

'Thank you.'

It was a relief to escape from him for a while. To stand up to the Ians of the world one needed a stouter pair of legs than she possessed. She swayed and urgently gripped the washbasin. Her dizzy spell lasted for only a moment. As soon as she was sufficiently recovered, she held her wrists under the cold water tap, and splashed her face. How good it felt, tingling cold and reviving.

Her hand went up to the ledge above the washbasin in a gesture that was purely automatic. But her searching fingers met nothing, because there was nothing on the ledge for them to meet.

It came home to her, for perhaps the first time, just how much she had lost, how much had gone up in flames. Her luggage, her handbag, filled with all those trivial possessions that are so much a part of a woman's way of life. A phial of perfume, carefully saved for very special occasions. The tortoise-shell comb, stamped with her own personal initials. Her lipstick.

She began to cry then, the tears came splashing hurriedly down her cheeks, all because she didn't own a lipstick. She was suffering, not from shock, but from an overdose of emotionalism. It had all happened too quickly, and had been a bit too much. And to cap it all, her best friend was her enemy.

I will not drive that dratted car. I will not, not, not. I will tell him to go to blazes before I will get in that car and drive.

But he was in the driving seat. He was in the driving seat! She was almost beside herself with elation and she ran across the forecourt, stumbling and almost tripping herself up in her eagerness to occupy the passenger seat. Before he did.

Ah! Heavenly not to have to handle awkward, unfamiliar gears, not to have to think, listen to directions, not to have to wait, watch and anticipate.

'Oh, by the way,' he said, overplaying the casual touch. 'There's something in the glove compartment that belongs to you.'

'To me? To me?' The glove compartment was operated by a small button. She pressed it. The flap fell forward, and Darling Ugly fell into her lap.

CHAPTER FIVE

The troll doll was back in her pocket again. Now she'd got it back, things must start coming right again. She'd loved it, and examined it, and run her fingers through its abundance of coarse, orange hair. And then put it away, where it belonged, yet still keeping her fingers pressed against the slight bulge in her dress pocket.

'I see you had to operate.'

'A stitch here, a stitch there.' He flashed her a brief deprecatory smile. 'Nothing really. I'm only sorry he's not in mint condition for your sake. Poor little chap got a bit trampled on. I almost didn't see him.'

'I'm so pleased you did.'

First examination had revealed a line of exquisite stitches encircling the doll's right ear. She didn't know which delighted her most, the doll's safe return, or the thoughtfulness that had been sewn into every stitch.

Her head went back on the leather upholstery. It was nice to be out of the driving seat, in more than the literal sense. She hadn't made a very good job of directing her own life and, for the moment at least, she was happy to sign away her independence and let someone else take charge. And, although he aggravated her, and at times she almost hated him—not almost, did!—she was glad that someone was Ian Nicholson.

The road zigzagged and turned, it had more twists in it than a corkscrew, it frequently disappeared, but always popped up again. Karen grew sleepy watching it. She thought,

I've been having a reaction and this is the soporific afterwards.

In all, the ride lasted no more than twenty minutes. She tried to keep her ears alert for Ian's occasional commentary, and her lids up for the scenic attractions. The road was hedged in by fields, with steep paths sloping off in all directions. A farmhouse was stencilled, artistically, against the skyline; her view of it was abruptly cut off by the meandering road and they were careering through a dark ravine of trees, a canyon of a million sounds, leaves chuckled and whispered, they were so thickly pressed together there wasn't a chink or a parting to let in the light. The road danced into the dazzle of the sun before they did, curving and leaping in rapid descent.

A number twenty-nine bus passed them, making heavy weather of lumbering up the road they had glided so effortlessly down. Karen filed this piece of information without being conscious of doing so. If she wished to keep her tentative date with Mitch, the bus was the obvious means of transport.

A house slid into view, then another, and another. This was the new and fashionable part of town. Each house was architect designed and completely unrelated to its neighbour. Wide, open lawns swept down to the road. Beyond the shops the dwellings began to lose in artistry and gain in character.

The little brown houses, some with mullioned windows and thatched roofs, nestled in dreamy tranquillity.

The road began to do erratic things again, namely vanish into a wood of tall pines. Unlike the other times it did not reappear, and then Karen spotted the stone gates. Ian drove through them, along a short drive, and stopped before a house that was a big cousin to the little brown houses.

She was almost too tired to voice her delight. She tried, but only managed a croak, in any case she needed her energy for walking.

The door, under a triangular porch, was inches thick. It groaned open to reveal a family room, with comfortable deep brown chairs. A yellow jug, filled with flowers, made a bright splash of colour on the wide, cottage-style sill. Beyond an open archway, stairs curved away and upwards. At the top was a long passage with three doors. On each door, at eye level, was an oval plaque, for easy identification. Pipe and slippers on the first plaque, bath and shower on the second, overnight suitcase on the third.

The overnight guest room had white walls. It was simply furnished with a chest of drawers, a dressing table with a tall slim mirror, a single wardrobe, a divan bed, and a bedside table with a shelf containing an assortment of books. The wall to wall carpet was old gold, and this colour was picked up in the gold and white striped curtains and bedspread.

Ian pointed to the bed. 'Into there with you. I'll bring you up a cup of tea. And then you can have a nice long sleep.'

She took off her dress and hung it in the wardrobe. It looked ridiculous and slightly forlorn hanging there on its own. She didn't remember Ian bringing up the tea, but when she awoke, a long time later, it was on the bedside table. Untouched and, she tasted, cold.

She lay for a minute trying to pull in her thoughts. Because her tidy mind was in an untidy stupor, she tried to number them, thinking that way they might make better sense. One: She had made a proper hash of things. Two: She trusted Ian Nicholson implicitly. Considering, number two was a nice thought. Three: She couldn't accept his charity. Four: For the time being she had no alternative but to accept his charity. Five: He attracted her more than any man she had ever met. Not visually, although he was worthy of a second look, but in the physical sense.

Oh, go away, thought number five. The situation, as it stood, was bad enough, without that complication.

What an idiot she'd been. If only she'd insured full comprehensive and not just third party. If only she hadn't been driving on the wrong side of the road. If only her father hadn't met Angela. If only . . . oh dear, she was overworking those two small words, but! If these things hadn't happened, she wouldn't be here now. And though nine-tenths of her wished to be anywhere but there, the remaining one tenth was extremely happy with the outcome.

She had a quick wash, put on her dress, and ventured downstairs. At first she thought the big room was empty, until a quiet voice said:

'That was some sleep.'

This lovely old house must have got to work on him. He was mellowed, warmer, humbled, approachable. She blinked. 'Yes, it was.'

He abandoned the papers he had been working on, closed the writing desk, and crossed the room to lift her chin with a careless thumb and forefinger to examine her face critically.

'Yes, a decided improvement. Come and sit down. And talk.'

'What about?'

'About us. Living in the same house, until we decide what to do with you, without causing village eyebrows to stir. You know in London, in Leeds even, we could live together without causing comment. But in Hamblewick . . .? No, it definitely isn't on.'

She sat in one of the deep brown armchairs, he perched on a low stool, his hands dangled loosely between his hunched up knees, his head was slightly on one side, deeply considering.

'They are nice people, all of them. Not a bigot among them, but their horizon is very narrow, and consequently they think small. And, another consideration, I don't want you to be hurt. The nicest people do tend to have gossipy tongues.'

She hadn't considered the moral aspect of the situation. Since waking up in hospital, a paralysing lassitude had possessed her, cross-graining her sense of right and wrong, depriving her of wider reasoning. What did he mean? What was he trying to tell her? That he had brought her here on impulse, but now that he'd had time to chew the matter over, he realized she couldn't stay. She said promptly:

'Of course, I'll move out.'

Anyway, it was only a temporary situation. At best a patched roof that would soon let in the rain.

He eyed her keenly. She seemed such a small person, weighted down with such a heavy load of gloom.

'No. There is a way you can stay put and not offend Willie Smith, the butcher, Pat Dawlish, post mistress cum grocer and confectioner, Alan and Alice Newby, newsagents, Mrs Bramwell, and uncle Tom Cobley and all.'

'Who's Mrs Bramwell?' she enquired, her mouth copying his and turning up at the corners.

'The old dear who does my laundry.'

'You certainly wouldn't want to offend her!'

'Do you like my home?' Her eyebrows went up at the random question.

'I do,' he said, barely giving her chance to nod. 'I've always had a feeling for old houses, and when I inherited this one from my grandmother, I knew I had to live here. Despite the difficulties, I couldn't sell; it would be like selling a part of my childhood. I'm in the export business, by the way.' He tossed that in wryly, as if it should explain the urge that had prompted him to hang on to his country residence.

'Have you seen the tele ad: the big thief, a past master at delegation, with that extra sense of perception vital for pulling off brilliant deals without turning a hair. Well, that's not me. I don't miss many tricks, but it's slog, drive, graft all the way. This is where I come to rest my ulcers.'

Her lips rushed from a gentle smile into a full-blown laugh. 'You haven't got ulcers.'

'How would you know?' he said.

'Because it would show in your face. Tiny suffering lines. Here and there.' Her fingers traced an outline, but carefully did not touch. Heeding her brain's awakened warning. Inflammatory. Look, but don't permit contact.

'All right, so I don't have ulcers. But I suffer. And this is my piece of accessible heaven. The place I come to untie the tension knots and cast out the conflict.'

'And does it?'

'Yes. But to go back to Mrs Bramwell.'

'The lady who does your laundry?'

'The very one. Well, I've approached her to come in daily, to dust and do a spot of cooking. But Horace, that's her husband, strongly objects to his wife taking on more work, which leaves me foraging for myself, and I wondered . . . seeing as you are at a loose end? Anyway, think it over for a moment. The house isn't quite as it was in my grandmother's day. Besides doing a bit of work on the interior, I had the stables converted into a garage and had an extra bedroom put in the stable loft. If you did stay to housekeep for a while, until you find your feet, I'd move in there.'

'Couldn't I move into the stable accommodation? Then I wouldn't feel as if I was turfing you out.'

'No, because you see I've asked Val Stainburn to come down. She'll be company for you. And besides that, Val will make an excellent chaperon.'

He sounded so serious that she found it necessary to quell an impulse to laugh, and absorbed herself in pretending to turn over his recent proposition. In fact, she was wondering what he was getting at. Did his eyes mock, or was it her imagination? He did have splendid eyes—they mocked and condemned so beautifully, that it was almost worth engendering his disapproval. But she mustn't let herself be mesmerised, or side-tracked by superfluous, and blatantly untrue, thoughts. Let him reserve his dark looks for someone else, someone with a back strong enough to ride them. She'd settle for, would willingly perform a backward somersault for, a grain of his approval. But this line of thought wasn't furthering her cause. What other possibilities? Was he ribbing her? Hinting that she was a child of yesterday's generation, who wouldn't feel safe unless chaperoned? And had he been so certain of her acceptance that he'd already asked this person to come down!

'Who is Val Stainburn?' she enquired an inspired moment later.

'A friend. Also a business colleague.' His voice was curiously toneless, giving nothing away. 'We shall be at work for the greater part of each day. I hope you won't be lonely.'

'I'll try not to be. Anyway, I shall have my domestic duties. Oh!' Her hand went up to her mouth, smothering the gasp. 'I hope you didn't get the wrong impression when I said I kept house for my father. The truth is, I'm not very competent. Father said it was because I lacked concentration. I think it's just too wonderful of you, asking your friend down so that I won't feel compromised, and everything, and I promise to concentrate really hard.'

His mouth straightened out and he looked distinctly uncomfortable.

'Look, I do need a housekeeper, so forget all that wonderful rot. And the first thing I want you to concentrate on is getting well. You know, your recent ordeal took its toll.'

'Yes . . . yes, I believe it did.'

His tongue was no longer saturnine, hadn't been all evening for that matter, and now, even though his face was tormented by a whiplash of unease, it was still warmly compassionate.

'When does Miss Stainburn arrive?' she enquired.

Not only did the name signal a frown, but his tone cooled and became so remote it could have travelled via satellite.

'Tomorrow.'

Why? Why so cold, so curt? She remembered his thoughtfulness in stitching Darling Ugly. If this was another kind of thoughtfulness, it was unnecessary. She knew, as Miss Stainburn wasn't arriving until tomorrow, they would be unaccompanied tonight; she didn't need that fact underlining, just as he didn't need to erect a stone wall, not for her benefit. Despite odd skirmishes with fate, her faith in human nature was still reasonably intact. Even her father's offhand treatment, one of the darker grey skirmishes, had not seriously diminished it. And, everything apart, she felt secure and trusting where Ian was concerned. Unless it was a deliberate measure, so that she wouldn't get any wrong ideas!

Oh! Could that be it! Her hand moved up again, to stem a second exclamation, and a blush shamed her cheeks. Mercifully his back was to her as he said: 'I'll move my things into the room over the garage. Then we'll have supper.'

Supper was a constrained meal. Ian was thoughtful, and she, in humiliation, couldn't think of anything to say.

After the meal, Ian bade her goodnight. She locked the door after him. Now that she was alone she began to think, not only about the present, but the future. If only she could lift up the edge of tomorrow and take a small look. A trickle of self-pity crept in. After all, this housekeeping job could only be a stop-gap. And then what? Should she write to her father? For more money? But that must be the last resort. She didn't want to have to tell him what a foolish girl she'd been; besides, he'd prefer to spend what spare cash he had on Angela. Which wasn't much. He was going through a lean period, unless his luck had changed since her departure, and, considering, he had been as generous as he was able to be. So that left her standing on her own insubstantial, cotton-wool legs.

Ian was right. The accident had taken its toll. She didn't feel as good as she usually did. She ached inside and out, and oh it had been so nice talking to Ian, the mellowed Ian, even though the sweetness of it had almost ripped her in two.

Oh, why had he changed so suddenly, reverted right back to type? When she wanted more; more kindness, more soft kitten comfort.

The telephone rang. She considered not answering it. It couldn't be for her. It rang three times and then stopped. She wished she'd answered it. Five minutes elapsed, then it rang again.

'Hello,' she said.

'Karen, is that you?'

For a moment she wondered if Ian had a line rigged up from the garage to the house. She said: 'Yes, it's me,' and held her breath.

A chuckle carried down the line. 'I didn't think it was old Ian. You're staying at the house, then? I did wonder . . . are you alone?'

'Quite alone. Who is that?'

'Don't you know? Can't you guess?'

'No, I can't,' she snapped. 'Please stop teasing.'

'Sorry, didn't mean to. It's Mitch.'

What did he mean by, 'Are you alone?' Was he hinting at anything? Ian's manner, his calculated coolness, had triggered off a reaction in her. Her brain teemed with thoughts, making her brand 'suspect' what might have been kindly motive, impelling her to explain: 'It's all very correct, I assure you, so you can stop wondering. Ian—' (Should that have been Mr Nicholson?) 'has engaged me as his housekeeper. Since you thought it worth while to check up on me, I'll repeat. I am alone, quite, quite alone. Ian has moved into the premises over the garage.'

'Sweet porcupine, I'm not checking up on you. I phoned on the off chance you might be there. That's all. I swear it. And I'm certain Ian will make a praiseworthy employer. But if you want a reference, go along and see the vicar of St Mary's. He's known him almost as long as I have, and it will make the old boy feel useful.'

'Don't be irreverent,' she reproved, still feeling raw. And, anyway, she had been taught to respect the cleric.

'Sorry,' came the contrite reply. 'But I don't want to talk about Ian.'

'What did you want to talk about? If you weren't checking up on me, why did you ring? Anything special?'

'Very special. I wanted to say goodnight.'

At the moment Howard Mitchell was a salesman. The first thing a good salesman learns to sell is himself, and though a comparative newcomer to the business, he had the qualities of a very good salesman. It has been said he could sell milk to a dairymaid, if not to a dairyman.

'That's very sweet of you, Mitch.' Sweet, because it's what she had craved for all evening. Just a small spoonful of friendship, lightly flavoured with affection.

'Not sweet. Selfish. I shall take your voice to bed with me. Did you know you have the dulcet tones of a singer. Have you ever sung, professionally I mean?'

'No. I do sing, but only for my own pleasure.'

'I hope some day you'll let me share that pleasure. Are you relaxed now? Not tense and all screwed up like a ball of twine any more?'

'How did you know?'

'I inherited the clear sight from my perspicacious grandmother. It told me there was a little girl who needed cheering up. And now . . . goodnight, little girl.'

Ian came out of the Woodpecker, one of Hamblewick's two pubs, whistling the tune the girl guitarist had been strumming. It was an evening ritual, one drink, pleasant conversation. He got on well with the locals, who had known him on and off since he was a lad. He lit a last cigarette, enjoying the peace of the unlit lane.

The cottage was in darkness. Good. She needed an early night. He wondered what Val would make of her, and what she would make of Val. He also wondered if he could sneak some papers out of the desk without waking her.

No, it was too late. If she did wake she might think someone had broken in to commit burglary. He paused where the drive split in two, and was just about to turn to his own quarters when the scream hit the night. His immediate thought was that someone had broken in. His key clicked into the lock and he took the stairs at two and three a time. As he thrust open the door, the landing light splashed in ahead of him, illuminating her bed, her shaking shoulders, her glazed, terror stricken eyes.

She was sitting bolt upright, sobbing and screaming, and it was like nothing he had ever heard before. He grasped her by the upper arm and said her name, over and over again, trying to release her from the turgent grip of whatever nightmarish horror possessed her.

She became aware of his presence and stopped screaming to look at him. Her mouth was still in the shape of a scream and the pupils of her eyes were wild and dilated.

'You promised you wouldn't leave me alone . . . but you did, you did. You knew I'd be frightened . . . it hurts . . . please take it away . . . the pain . . . I can't stand the pain.'

He'd thought, for a moment, that she was awake. Now he realized she was still in the dream, the nightmare.

'Where is the pain?' he asked.

She whimpered: 'You know where it is.'

'No, I don't. You must tell me.'

'It's . . . it's . . . the pain is here.'

She drew a line from the base of her throat to the hollow between her breasts. And the line stayed as a livid pinkness, a burn scar that hadn't yet faded. But she hadn't been burned in the car accident. Bruised, shocked, covered in mud. But not burned.

'I've taken the pain away,' he said. 'It's gone.'

'Gone,' she repeated dully. 'Gone.'

Her body relaxed, grew languorous. He began to enjoy the fragrant nearness of her, the soft feel of the satin skin beneath his fingers, and he knew it was time to go.

CHAPTER SIX

On waking, the first thing she noticed was the butcher blue and white striped pyjama jacket folded across the foot of the bed. It had not been there last night. She buttoned it on, and listened to the creak on the stair.

'Anyone for breakfast? Do you like boiled eggs?' His head poked round the door. 'I've done you two.'

'I love boiled eggs. I didn't expect waiter service.'

'Nor will you get it,' he said. 'After today. I don't cosset my housekeepers. I expect them to cosset me. Did you sleep well?'

'M-m. Lovely, thank you.' She was cracking the top of her egg and smiling up at him. She knew nothing about the nightmare. He wondered if he should mention it, but the last few weeks had bowled her nothing but shocks and he felt that now wasn't the time to ferret and probe, not while she was vulnerable from sleep. Perhaps later, perhaps never, if it proved to be an isolated incident. What had terrified her? Marked her flesh? And had she come to accept her disfigurement, or was it a still painful subject?

'You'd better do some personal shopping today,' he said. 'Here's some money.'

'It's too much,' she said, reluctant to touch the proffered notes.

'No, it's not. You'll need a coat.'

'It's still summer. What do I need a coat for?'

'You'll find out. This is England, remember. Buy a couple of dresses, and a cardigan. Oh, and,'—his eyes charged past hers and chased up the wall—'a nightgown and a pair of bedroom slippers. But you'll know what you need.' His glance seemed to be fixed on the ceiling, his mouth wore a peculiar kind of smile. 'If there's anything left over, call at the butcher's and get three decent sized fillet steaks for supper.'

She left off examining his expression to examine the money, maintaining a mute and stony silence. Still enjoying his own private joke, he tucked it under the brown earthenware marmalade jar. 'Buy the meat locally. I like to support local tradespeople

69

whenever I can. You'll need to go farther afield for any decent clothes. I'd recommend Todbridge, that's where we had lunch yesterday. Number twenty-nine bus, on the hour. The bus stop is outside the post office. Any comments?'

'Yes. What the heck are you smirking at?'

'Smirking? Smirking? Who's smirking?' His lips smacked into a frown.

'You were.' She eyed him suspiciously, but he was on guard now and showed her his saturnine countenance. She willingly abandoned the probe to ask:

'Did your grandmother possess a sewing machine?'

'I wouldn't know. She may have. She thriftily made up her own curtains, so it's more than a possibility. I disposed of some of her stuff, but not a sewing machine. If it's anywhere, it'll be in the attic.'

'Mind if I root? I'm not professional enough to make a coat, but I could manage a couple of nighties, and some undies. Perhaps even a dress.'

'You don't have to. I can let you have some more money if that isn't enough. I'm not hard up.'

'No, but I am. And I can only accept an amount I can pay back. It must be a loan. I promise to pay back every penny.' She was immutable, mindless in her determination to pay back the loan.

70

'All right. All right.' He hadn't time to argue. 'I must go in to work today. I'll see you this evening. And—good rooting.'

When he had gone she looked at the money as if it was something that might bite. She had to take it, she couldn't go about looking like Eve; but it was abhorrent to her to borrow. Although it was disloyal of her to think it, her adored father was a man of flexible principles, and even he wouldn't borrow. He was quite illogical on the subject. He would steal, accept a gift, or do without, but he wouldn't borrow. To do something he wouldn't stoop to, made her seem less of a person. She hadn't minded accepting the gift of clothes from Ian, she didn't mind eating his food. But she did mind picking up that money.

She thought it might be dusty grubbing about in the attic, and shrank from going up there in her one and only dress. She wondered if she could fix it with her conscience to 'steal' one of Ian's old shirts.

The master bedroom was about four times the size of hers. Three windows paced one wall, giving it an unsurpassed vista of trees in soldierly ranks, marching in dark, menacing majesty towards a rough heather clad fell that rose out of the blackness and the gloom in a series of humps to a skyline softened with cloud.

The view was such that it dominated all conscious thought, and she felt her breath catch imperceptibly in her throat and wished she had her father's skill with a brush and pallette. She had his eye and his off-beat appreciation of beauty, but not his clever fingers. The sharply contrasting contours, too vivid for some tastes, stirred her senses and for a moment she was haunted by the strange loveliness, possessed almost by other spirits who in earthly form had clung to this window and enjoyed the merging of the obvious prettiness of pinky mauves, violets and greens, and thrilled at, and perhaps experienced a chilling feeling of disquiet by, the enveloping darkness and pagan density of the woodland.

It was almost an anti-climax to turn away and examine the room. It was so normal and ordinary; huge wardrobe units filled the deep chimney alcoves and a pastoral scene, idyllic and timeless and pleasing to the eye, adorned the white wall. It was a simple watercolour. Karen liked it. It did not inspire her to depths of feeling, and she did not know if she liked it because of, or in spite of this. She was still searching, finding out about herself through the medium of art appreciation.

The candlewick bedspread was cornflower blue, several old-fashioned hooky rugs in variegated shades of blue, from cornflower to deep wedgewood, set off the mellow beauty of the waxed, elm floor.

Investigation showed that Ian had emptied one unit of furniture completely, obviously to make room for his guest's clothes. Would Miss Stainburn like this room? As she rested her elbows on the sill would she be filled with reckless exhilaration? Or would she back away from the pressing nearness of the trees? What kind of a person was she?

Karen moved to the other unit of furniture. The mahogany gleamed blood-red as the heavy door swung back to reveal a tie rack and several drawers. His shirts were in the third drawer down. She found a checked one in peacock-blue and green. Perfect for her purpose. She was just about to take her spoils and go when she spotted the photograph of a petite girl sandwiched between two tall men. The girl was not pretty, not obviously pretty, but Karen sensed an elusive something ready to penetrate the elfin features and wide apart eyes. The men were also unsmiling. It was the Ian she knew best, saturnine and half in profile. The other man was staring blankly at the camera, as if waiting for someone to say 'cheese' before troubling to fix his features. Perhaps that was why she didn't immediately realize it was Mitch. She knew Mitch's face best in smile, perhaps because she didn't want to remember him looking bleak and slaughtered. It didn't look a very old photo, the corners weren't curled and it wasn't sepia with age, so that meant the breach between them couldn't be very old either. Had they quarrelled over the girl? And was Valerie

Stainburn small, with elfin features?

The sewing machine was in the darkest corner of the attic. She disturbed a spinning spider to brush it reasonably free of dust, and then carried it gingerly down to the living room, where she soon had it wheezing into action. She experimented on her new acquisition, Ian's shirt, slicing off the tail and hemming it round, shortening the sleeves and generally adapting it to her requirements. Presto, she had a knock-about shirt dress.

She would have changed back into her green dress, but she left herself short of time. As it was she had to leg it to the bus stop. It was market day in Todbridge and Karen was fascinated by the huddle of open stalls. She found one selling material and bought two dress lengths, a multi-coloured print and a matt cream that handled beautifully and would lend itself to dressing up. At another stall she bought knitting wool in a pretty russet shade, needles and a cardigan pattern, selected because of its uncomplicated stitch.

Then she went back to the first stall because she'd forgotten to look for lingerie material. She found some remnant pieces and because they were so cheap she planned to make two underskirts, and three shortie nighties with high drawstring necklines and tiny puffed sleeves.

'Replenishing your wardrobe?'

She swung round and grinned up at Howard

Mitchell. 'You make it sound a chore,' she accused. 'It's fun!'

He grimaced. 'Only a woman could say that. Have you had enough fun for today? Or might I tear you away for a spot of lunch?'

'You might. My thoughts were already edging that way.'

'You mean you accept. You'll let me buy your lunch?'

'Why shouldn't I?' she counter-questioned his incredulity. 'You might have quarrelled with Ian, but you and I have no axe to grind. You saved my life; in the circumstances I should treat you to lunch.'

'I won't hear of that,' he said, much to her delight as she didn't want to get too heavily indebted to Ian, and she would have had to use his money to pay for her fine gesture.

'But are you sure?' he persisted. 'I'm sorry to be such a Doubting Thomas, but are you sure? What will Big Brother say?'

'Nothing. For the simple reason that I shan't tell him.'

His chuckle was low and resonant as his hand nipped easily into the crook of her elbow to guide her through the stalls.

'Know what I do first thing every morning?'

'Open your eyes?'

'Ah! So I'm squiring a joker, am I?' he said. 'After I've opened my eyes, after I've washed and shaved, before I have breakfast, know what I do?'

'No, what?'

'I read my horoscope. Know what my horoscope said this morning?'

'No, but—' She suppressed a giggle. 'My stars! I'm going to!'

'It said—and I will ignore the flippancy— today you meet your destiny.'

'It didn't!'

He grinned. 'No, it didn't. Actually it said "Good phase for exchanging information and pooling ideas with a comparatively new friend." Well, new friend, to begin. I'm thirty-one, in unsettled employment, and I dislike wearing odd socks. That's enough information to be going on with. My idea, at the moment, is to know you much better. Now it's your turn.'

'My turn?'

'Dear Dimwit, your turn to exchange information and pool ideas. I never let my horoscope down.'

'Now you're being flippant,' she accused. 'Are you a disbeliever?'

'M-m.' His expression was dead-pan. 'Let's put it this way. I never walk under a ladder, or on a crack, if I can help it. And I never, but never whistle in a dressing room. Now, about lunch. What's it to be. A sit down in a restaurant, or pot luck with traveller's samples?'

'Pot luck, please,' she answered promptly. 'Are you a traveller?'

'For my sins, yes,' he said, his voice

unfolding in a bored drawl.

'Temporarily. Until I discover the crock of gold.'

'Oh that,' she pooh-poohed. 'Everybody's searching. Nobody finds.'

'I almost did once.'—Now the drawl conveyed a world of regret. 'I really thought I'd hit it good.'

'You know,' she teased. 'The streets aren't paved with gold. That's only a fallacy. They're paved with lost chance.'

He weighed her words, made nothing of them that pleased him, and for reply thrust out his lower lip like a thwarted child. She deduced he bitterly regretted his lost chance, and, on that subject at least, had put up a closed sign. What she had thought was pie in sky, was ambition, and he wasn't prepared to expose it to humorous banter. She pressed hurriedly for a change of subject, one less hazardous, and happily the mood of zany amiability was restored.

On the way to the car they stopped to shop for items not to be found in his samples. Bread rolls and butter, and a bag of crisp, sugar-glazed Eccles cakes.

Approaching the car park, Karen didn't have to grit her teeth. At first she was staggered, then relieved. Ian had done this for her. By bundling her straight back behind the wheel of a car, he had given her back her nerve. You have to relive an ordeal in order to conquer it. She just hoped there was one ordeal she wouldn't have to relive, even if she never conquered it.

Mitch was glancing across at her—doubtless remembering things too—trying to assess her reaction. She wanted to put out her hand and say, "It's all right". But it was enough to be all right. Anyway, she was so choked with relief, she doubted she had a voice.

'Into the yellow peril, with you,' he instructed. 'Let's hope we don't meet an exile from Europe. Don't worry,' he added. And in the mysterious manner of auto-suggestion, she immediately did begin to worry. 'We shan't meet up with anybody driving on the wrong side of the road. Lightning never strikes twice.'

He meant to be kind, but he couldn't have said anything more shattering. It was as if every syllable was spiked with a point of steel. She closed her eyes, and in memory heard the growl of thunder; yet it wasn't the thunder she feared, but its dread companion. Thunder might have the loudest voice, but it's lightning that has the power to sear and pain.

'Look, sweetie,' he said, abounding with grave consideration. 'You don't have to get in the car. There's a park nearby. We can have a meal alfresco style.' He elaborated invitingly: 'A picnic lunch. Won't that be fun? Much better than a stuffy old—'

'It's not the car. I'm all right,' she gulped.

'All right! All right, she says!' His hand

clapped across his forehead in exaggerated disbelief. 'After what you've been through, I'm a brute, a four headed monster for even suggesting . . . I mean, I should know better than anybody. I was there. I dragged you clear.' His sympathy washed over her like balm; she wallowed in it, she spread her arms in it, she tasted it in her mouth and savoured it on her tongue, and some of it trickled into her throat to thicken her voice. 'Do you mind if we get in the car and away from here. Before the flood gates open and I make a right spectacle of myself.'

She held back until they were parked in a quiet lane some three miles to the east of Todbridge. Then it was all up with her. A severely held barricade collapsed and she wept until there wasn't a tear left in her.

Mitch was marvellous in the role of comforter, administering soothing words, supplying her with a large clean handkerchief, her own being a useless, sodden, tightly screwed ball, offering her the use of his shoulder. His shoulder she declined, not without regret, because it looked wide and comfortable. But she had no intention of letting misery drive her into a man's arms. All the same she tried to convey her gratitude for his able handling of an unpleasant task. A regular envoy of mercy, light on tact perhaps, but offering sympathy with a lavish hand.

So kind of him. It wasn't his fault she felt

blotchy-eyed and wretched, and filled with self-loathing for creating such a scene. He was wonderful. She was tempted to confide all, the true reason for her conduct, but her misery made her maladroit and she couldn't be sure of finding the words. Besides which, enough is enough. So, contriving a light tone, she beseeched: 'Any chance of conjuring up some coffee? I've got a raging thirst.'

He produced a flask with the dexterity of a magician. He gave her his own pottery mug and he used the plastic vacuum flask cup.

'This is good,' she complimented. 'Did your wife make it for you?'

'I made it myself,' he said, answering only one part of her double edged question. 'Which is not quite what you wanted to know?'

'No,' she admitted unequivocally, even smiling at her own unabashed curiosity.

'No wife, Karen. The nearest I got was a fiancée.'

'But not any more?' No use falling at the first fence.

'She went away.'

'Oh.' Perhaps she should have fallen at the first fence, after all.

'A long way away. You could say she passed beyond the concept of wordly things.'

'I'm sorry.'

'Yes.' He knuckled his hands, bringing his thumbs together, holding on to something— thought? Reason? 'It was a bad business. She was too young to . . . too young.' His voice cracked mid sentence, died, came back with vigour. 'So you see, we share a common bond. We have both suffered. Shall we cheer one another up?' He was talking too loud, too fast, and his eyes were heavy with pain. He had suffered. The roles shifted. Now she was the comforter.

'I should like that,' she said gravely.

He countered: 'Ian won't approve.' His eyes narrowed. In taunt? Or speculation? All she knew was that at the mention of that name, some of the fire and vitality that had drained out of her, oozed back.

'I only work for him. My private life is my own. I don't defer to Ian, or anybody.'

His glance slanted in her direction. The pain had gone and was supplanted by a look of triumph, of undisguised caprice. It dried her mouth and gave her the feeling she had been cleverly manipulated to say just that.

'Let's eat now,' said Mitch, sending her an exquisite smile.

They did that. After which Mitch said, with sweet reluctance, that it was time to continue his rounds. She replied that she had some more shopping to do.

'Don't forget our date tomorrow,' he reminded.

'Is it still on? I didn't think you'd want to see me again, not so soon. And it was only a tentative arrangement to meet at Sharpe's.'

'On your part, maybe,' he charmed. 'There was nothing tentative about the arrangement in my mind. I want to see you again, now more than ever. The only thing I plan to change is the venue. Instead of Sharpe's, how about my collecting you in Hamblewick? I'm not suggesting charging the fortress,' he said, no doubt answering the slight lift of brow. 'I'll pick you up by the bridge.'

'Lovely,' she accepted. 'Please may I drive? Now, I mean, on the way back to Todbridge?'

His glance briefed her. It was levelled with disbelief, surprise, a hint of mischief. 'Have a heart, sweetie. My shoulder, yes. Anytime. But my car.' She felt like a chicken being inexpertly plucked alive. Something about her, the stiffening of her neck, or whatever flicked to her eye, engaged his attention and his voice dropped its teasing raillery and gathered compassion. 'Let's say,'—and who could deny this Mitch, forgiveness?—'I wouldn't put you through the agony.'

CHAPTER SEVEN

She completed the rest of her shopping in quick shakes, finding just the right all-purpose coat in the first shop she entered. It was camel, casual, warm for later, with the go-anywhere elegance of a higher priced garment. She

82

mitigated this extravagance by remembering the enormous saving made on the other necessary items. The purchase of a handbag presented a problem. Her depleted resources decreed a cheap plastic, but inclination rarely, if ever, endorses economy and yearned for soft leather. She loved the expensive feel of good leather, for handbag, gloves, shoes.

Unbeknown to her the wheels of compromise had ground into action. The very handbag her uneconomic heart lusted for lurked seductively in the Oxfam, nearly new shop. In the darkest corner, amid a pile of jumble. Real leather, well cared for by its previous owner, and price right.

Lipstick, foundation make-up, hairbrush (Woolworth's best), comb, toothbrush, home. How quickly she had come to think of Hamblewick as home. The money had spun out. She even had enough left over to buy mushrooms to garnish the steak.

The girl in the photo trotted in two paces behind Ian. Photographs lie. This girl was fairer, more elfin, thinner. An emaciated ghost with jutting cheekbones and bruised sparrow eyes. Karen cushioned her in the comfiest chair, and mentally fed her the largest steak. The one intended for Ian.

Ian introduced them. He said: 'Karen, I want you to meet Valerie Stainburn. Val, this is Karen Shaw. Karen has kindly consented to housekeep for me.'

The hand that rested for a brief moment in Karen's, felt stick brittle. She meant to say, 'How do you do,' but said: 'Have you been ill?'

The pointed chin bobbed up and down, but the grave little mouth remained sealed. It was left to Ian to explain: 'It's Val's first day back at work, after an absence of, oh—six months. The wanness is due to strain and apprehension. Getting back into harness, renewing old acquaintances and making new ones, can be nerve wracking. And I don't believe she had any lunch.'

'Then you must cat an enormous supper to compensate,' urged Karen, sounding as firmly established in the household as the clock on the wall.

'It's almost ready. You've just time to wash your hands. Bathroom, top of the stairs, second door on the left.'

Valerie said: 'I know where it is,' and vacated the room with little-girl docility. Karen's hands squared to her hips.

'Well?' she challenged Ian.

'Well what?' he countered, topping his voice up with caution, which tone butchered benefit of doubt thoughts and considerably stepped up her determination. 'Kindly explain,' she said tightly.

'M-m.' He gave her a shrewd, less wary glance, and came out of his corner. 'Val's been ill, is that what you mean? Desperately ill. She needs baby birding. I'm not asking you to

nurse her. I realize I engaged you as my
housekeeper and that your duties don't extend
to my guests. But I thought—'

'You thought! Oh, this is too laughable,' she
quibbled, unable to stay silent a moment
longer. 'Because I thought, but that's
unimportant now. What is important is the
role you've cast me as. Broody hen?' Her
tongue cavilled on, incensed beyond caution,
reason, or restraint. How could he have
tricked her? But he didn't, not really, upped
one renegade thought. He said he needed a
housekeeper. He went to great lengths to
impress he wasn't inventing the position. But
she hadn't believed him.

'What did you think?' he invited.

'I thought she was coming here to mother
hen me. Yes, I really thought you'd invited her
to cosset me.'

'Now you wouldn't want that,' he said
simply.

'How do you know what I want?' she said,
unappeased. 'And anyway, what are you
running here—a convalescent home?'

'No,' he retaliated. 'Nor a kindergarten. It
only seems that way. Now, stop behaving like a
spoilt brat and attend to supper. I've had one
heck of a day. Temperament would be the last
straw.'

'Why you . . . you . . . ' Her tongue wrapped
round something blistering and unrepeatable.
His eyes shrieked disapproval and for a

moment she thought he was going to warm her ears, but instead he threw back his head and he laughed. There is no more formidable weapon on earth than laughter, as, to her sorrow, she found out. Because it was frustration, not abuse, that scalded her throat and made her back to the kitchen.

She put him in mind of, not a mother hen, but an angry, spitting kitten. With her tight little mouth and her enraged emerald eyes. Kittens can be coaxed.

'Karen,' he humoured. 'Stop pretending. You know you're going to love playing at mothers. All little girls do. I won't make many conditions. Only two.' His laughing eyes, his quivering mouth, made fiction of his clamped serious tone. 'Plain English cooking, that means none of your paella. And kindly lay off my shirts. Although,'—now eyes, mouth and tone were in amused accord—'I admit, it never looked that good on me.'

When there is no ready reply to fence back, to exit with dignity is perhaps the best recourse. But it's hard to be dignified when, literally, wearing the shirt off your opponent's back. In the circumstances, Karen just did the best she could.

I won't be conned this way, she thought. I don't want to coddle his tragic girl friend. I don't want to keep house for him. And I won't. As soon as I'm able to, I'll pay back the money I've borrowed and then I'll be free to walk out.

And to blazes with the pair of them!

Now, how could she get her hands on a sizable sum of money, quickly? It struck her, as she sat on the tall kitchen stool hugging her bare knees, that she needed some of Mitch's philosophy, if not his mythical crock of gold.

As the time drew near, she wondered how best to keep her appointment with Mitch. She could face up to Ian and say boldly, 'Look, I know you dislike him. But that's nothing to do with me. Just because I eat your bread, it doesn't automatically follow that I also have to swallow your prejudices.'

Damn the man! He had unfair bias on his side. She did eat his bread. Damn him for making her feel disloyal for wanting to see Mitch. Talk to him, be charmed by him. Mitch was a pretty butterfly, put on earth to brighten a drab day. Not that it had been a drab day. She shopped, renewing her acquaintance with Willie Smith, the butcher. 'Was the steak tender yesterday? Yes, there's some veal in the fridge.' And becoming acquainted with Pat Dawlish, Hamblewick's gossipy postmistress and general store keeper, who greeted, with friendly lack of ceremony: 'Hello love. Younger than I expected. It's all right, I suppose,'—dubiously—'Yes, I reckon it's all right.' She spread her hands on the counter in a gesture of extreme propriety, and squared her prudish outlook by adding: 'He was that desperate. Apart from saddling himself with the responsibility of young Valerie—isn't that just like him?—he's not what you could call a man about the house type. Not tidy, nor given to sewing on buttons. And Martha Bramwell isn't getting any younger, otherwise I'm sure she'd go in, say twice a week. But she's her own house to follow. Then there's Horace, that's her husband, blethers every time she mentions charring. Begrudges her her bit of pin money, he does. Pin money, beer money for him more likely. Men really are the limit, aren't they? But then, you'll not have had the experience of them yet.' Even squared consciences can't resist priggish thrusts, and that last was that all right, plus fruity query. Collectively it was proof, if indeed she still required it, that he had needed a housekeeper. She must now reject quixotic notion and accept indisputable fact.

Inwardly seething, she decided it was politic to say nothing, and even firmly clamped the temptation to quiz Mrs Dawlish about 'young' Valerie. She was certain Ian didn't look upon her as a responsibility, not a burdensome one anyway.

'Sugar, flour, marge—you going to do a spot of baking, love?—dried fruit, matches,' said Pat Dawlish, checking the items off against the list. 'That's the lot.'

The village was more or less deserted when the yellow car pulled over the bridge. It was a warm evening, oppressive, the hot breath before the cooling downpour. Karen wished she'd had time to make up the luxurious cream material, but it was no farther than the cutting out stage. Shopping, cleaning, foraging, cooking, it all took time. Plain English, Ian had insisted upon. She supposed veal wasn't traditional, but, cooked in the special way her father liked, it was tasty. Valerie, sweetly appreciative, had overcome her shyness— shyness or mute antagonism—to pronounce it so.

As soon as the last plate had been washed and put away, Karen said she felt like a good long walk, and had escaped, with a delicious sense of playing truant.

'Nothing like a punctual girl,' approved Mitch, swinging open the car door to let her in. 'Shows eagerness. What have you been doing with yourself today?' She told him. It sounded dull and domesticated.

'No wonder the damsel is eager,' he grinned. 'Was it easy?'

'Not very. I'm not accomplished, you see.'

'At breaking out?'

She laughed. 'I thought you meant the cooking. Getting away was dead easy. I said I wanted to take a long walk and asked Val if she'd like to accompany me.'

'Val?'

'Valerie Stainburn.' She looked at him from under her lashes. 'She's been ill—but you'd know about that.'

'I would?' He flinched, as if he'd been struck, and added sharply:

'What's Ian been telling you?'

'Nothing. We don't discuss you. He doesn't know I'm with you now. I meant to tell him. But it's one thing to think bold, another to act it.'

His eyes grew frosty and she thought, 'What a coward he thinks I am.' She should have told Ian straight out. He couldn't have prevented her from coming. But it would have made the atmosphere worse than it already was, and so she had decided to say nothing.

'I find it hard to believe I haven't been under discussion, not after that accusation.' And she found it hard to believe it was Mitch talking. He sounded so polite and withdrawn and stiff.

'Accusation? What are you talking about? I said you would know. And I honestly thought you would. Look, we seem to be at cross purposes, so I'd better explain. I found a snap of you, Val and Ian, in one of the drawers. I assumed, as you were chummy enough to have your photo taken with her, you'd know her state of health.'

'Is that what . . . I thought . . . ?' He stopped mangling his knuckles to look at her. 'I don't know what I thought. I'm sorry I bit your head off, but don't do anything daft like that again.' He was so bashful and repentent that she forgave him his childish tantrum with the

90

utmost ease.

'What did I do daft?'

'Ask Val to come, when you know I want you all to myself.' His tone was seductive, flattering. She couldn't remember a time when flattery had been so appreciated; come to think of it, she'd almost forgotten how pleasant it was to be flattered.

'She might have accepted,' he added, keeping up the good work.

'No chance. She looked flaked out.' She chewed her little finger nail, and reflected: 'I thought it was rather clever of me.'

'Yes, yes it was.' He took her hand from her mouth, shook his head at the damaged nail, gave her back her hand. 'You did right not to mention my name. It would only put backs up, to no good purpose. A word in your ear, sweetie. Don't let Val take you in.' He began to say something, smothered it, and said instead: 'But she wouldn't. You've enough savvy to know whether a person's stable or not. Val can lie her little head off, she won't fox you. Ian, maybe. He's been brainwashed over a long period of time.'

She couldn't imagine anyone being wily enough to brainwash Ian, but she kept that thought to herself. The car spun over the bridge and away to the left, taking an unfamiliar road.

'What's it to be?' said Mitch. 'The flicks? Or a pub crawl?'

91

'Could we crawl into one pub and stay put? I don't want to be away too long.'

'One pub it is. The Grapes. That's where I take my best girls.'

It was a provocative remark, one that invited Karen to ask:

'Have there been many?'

'Enough,' he replied with truth, which gave his next remark the realism of a confidence imparted. 'Even though they do scare me.'

One didn't, she thought, remembering he'd once been engaged. His face was pensive again, and deeply thoughtful. Was he haunted by the ghost of his lost love?

The Grapes was off the beaten track, but worth the finding judging by the number of parked cars. The rooms were small, leading one into another. You could sit on a cane chair and drink, or wander, drink in hand.

Mitch wandered no farther than the piano. He sat on the piano stool and stroked his fingers over the keyboard. He played a few bars of one tune, broke off, began another, then he blended the first tune back in. He finished to applause. Someone at a corner table shouted: 'Come on, Mitch. Play something we know. Something we can sing to.'

'How's this?' he said, his long sensitive fingers picking up a familiar melody. It was one she also knew, and Karen joined in. Her voice was not strong, but because she was standing next to Mitch, the notes carried across to him, sweet and clear. Her voice was only average, but she sang with expression, using herself to the full. It's never enough to have just a voice. The quality of a singer depends on the something else. And she had that something. He'd known it, intuitively, the moment she opened her mouth in speech, and before that even. It was fate that had made it his car that had driven her into the ditch.

He believed it wasn't enough to have fate on your side, you have to have the flair, the insight, to recognize that it is so, and even that isn't enough. Because more important is timing; having the patience and tact to wait for the right moment. And now, with her eye rushing to the clock on the wall, wasn't the right moment. It wasn't anything that could be hurried. He wanted time on his side, time to soak up her reactions, the first reaction to any project is not always the favourable, the acceptable one.

She had enjoyed herself so much that she was shocked to see how many minutes had been shaved off. He was tuned in to her wavelength. He leaped to his feet, and said, while she was still collecting the thought:

'I'll take you home. Before the storm breaks.'

CHAPTER EIGHT

Darling Ugly sat on her dressing table, watching her undress, his head for ever on one side, where he had been stitched.

When she was lonely, or unsure, or just plain scared, she talked to him. She said stupid, dotty things to him, but being a doll, he never so much as blinked an eye, but grinned back in friendly, some might say grotesque, fashion.

'I like Mitch,' she informed the troll. 'An hour with him doesn't flog me, emotionally. I'm relaxed, my nerve ends don't get the shakes.' With Mitch she didn't have to work at anything, didn't have to resist or yield, could just be herself. On the whole, people were a disappointment, in so much as they used her. She had nothing against being used, life is made up of loving . . . wanting . . . using. It was just that nobody used her in the way she wanted to be used.

Did anybody love her? want her? In his own way her father had loved her; and wanted her—as a menial, a domestic. She had cooked for him when he was hungry, talked to him when he was lonely. Ian wanted her in much the same way, because Mrs Bramwell's husband wouldn't let her char for him, and because he needed a pair of feminine hands to coddle Val. It was the pattern over again. When he had no further use for her, he would discard her, as her father had done.

But surely, she thought, I've been put on earth to give service as a woman? It must be nice—she tumbled into bed, throwing off most of the bedclothes—to be wanted as a woman.

She couldn't sleep. It was so hot. That wasn't the reason she couldn't sleep. Her bones had grown used to a warm climate, but not to a thunder menaced, lightning blighted sky. She shivered under the single cover as lightning cast its white whip at the sky, in swift successive strokes, soaking the tiny room in glare and then flinging it into vivid darkness. Dramatic black, violent white, with a simultaneous smash of thunder shuddering on the breath of the wind.

The rain came, it could be seconds or hours after, she couldn't tell. It fell like a curtain of tears, it drove away the death black and the hell white, it obliterated the shuffling sound of the wind, and the nonsensical noises, the screams and the moans in her throat. Or perhaps she just stopped screaming and moaning, because now she was conscious of a presence in the room.

A voice said softly: 'Are you all right?'

'I will be in a tick.' It came to her with swift certainty that the sibilant tone was male. 'Don't you dare put on the light,' she shrieked.

'I wasn't going to,' came the mild reply.

There followed a pause with a breath in it, like a prelude. All bedroom scenes should have pauses and romantic preludes, Karen thought.

The voice said: 'Can I stay awhile?'

'I'd rather you went away,' she said, stepping out of character, because didn't the heroine usually huskily acquiesce?

'You don't mean that,' he said, and Karen realized, sickeningly, that he wasn't going away. 'I do, I do,' she retorted. 'I hate you because I'm terrified of lightning.'

'That doesn't make sense.' He sounded puzzled. His foot steadied on the carpet, progress was slow, but assuredly he was advancing.

'It does to me. I want to see myself through my eyes. Not yours. You despise me. In that condescending way of yours, you'll try to jolly me round. But it isn't a joke, nor is it imaginary. It's real. It can touch you and hurt you. I know what I'm talking about.'

The shadowy form that was Ian, now stood by the bed. 'I'm not disputing that fact for a moment. But you're wrong on one count. I don't despise you. On the contrary, I admire you. You're about the bravest girl I know, and if you'd like to talk about it, I'll listen. If not we'll talk about something else.'

It was so unexpected, words failed her. The prepared ones, the come-out-fighting ones, were useless in the face of his turn-about kindness, and understanding.

'You're horrible,' she said, covering her eyes with her hands, though she didn't need to because it was a moonless night and quite dark.

'I'm sorry you think so.' His voice was not sarcastic, neither did it shake with laughter. 'Mind telling me why?'

'You're inconsistent,' she snapped. 'That's why. And it's incontestably horrid of you to be so kind. Anyway,'—a thought nipped in and set her brain ticking over—'What are you about? Prowling like a tomcat?'

'Not what you think.'

'Didn't the nasty storm wake up little Valerie?'

'Now who's being horrid?' His voice was tight and condemning, and for her this was familiar ground, ground she had thorough knowledge of and was acceptable because of this. She allowed: 'Yes, I suspect I am being pretty vile. I shall hate myself tomorrow. I didn't mean what you thought I meant, even though I said it to sound like that. I'm sure your motives are always as pure as a snowdrift.'

'Take out the always,' he said drily, 'and that reads about right. My motives are pure on this occasion. To always have pure motives would be untenable, and I'm not sure I don't mean downright impossible.'

If there had been a candle-glimmer of light in the room, their glances would have tangled,

97

but there wasn't, and so they didn't. Karen was incalculably glad, because, providing he was quick enough and astute enough, he might have read something for him in her eyes, whereas she was pretty certain she would have read nothing for her in his.

Oh, why don't you hurry up and go, she thought. Everything that should be said has been said. You heard me moaning and rightly assumed the storm had upset me, but it's passed over now. I can barely hear the rain. It's stopped rattling tin cans on the roof, and it's only a whisper on the window pane. I'm all right. Correction: as right as I'll ever be. What ails me, you wouldn't want to put right. So please go.

She closed her eyes. When she opened them there was no shadowy form by the bed.

* * *

Valerie, who not only looked like a bird, but ate like one as well, pushed aside her plate. 'I'm sorry,' she said. 'I can't eat any more.'

'Suit yourself,' said Karen indifferently. There was slightness and slightness, and if the girl wanted to walk about looking like a dehydrated sparrow, that was her own business. She was about to whisk away the plate, when the newspaper shielding the third occupant at table, lowered.

'Can't you manage just one mushroom

98

more?' coaxed Ian.

The fair hair was worn this morning in two bobs. Combine that with a sunshine yellow print, and you have an impression of the original urchin. The urchin mouth was woefully straight, until Ian spoke, and then it lifted at the corners to electrifying effect. Not quite dispelling plainness; but overstamping the whole with a beauty that was ethereal, volatile, even now the smile was breaking up and beginning to evaporate, but there stayed an impression of sweetness. The lines of the face were as they were before Ian intervened, but it was a different face, or perhaps Karen was seeing it in a different light, seeing the face as Ian saw it.

'I'm not much of a hand at breakfast, Ian,' Val explained, casting down her eyes and sounding like a child, heart-trippingly anxious not to offend. Too abasing, thought Karen, feeling her mouth pinch. Ian thought not.

'I know, chicken,' he said. 'You'll have to eat a big lunch. Otherwise, you'll disappear.'

'I'll try .. but.'

'I know you will. And to eliminate the but, I'll personally supervise.'

'But, Ian. You're so busy. And, besides, I feel a dreadful nuisance as it is.'

'You are that,' he said, his mouth wearing an overcoat of humour. Karen had never seen it put on more than a light jacket for her. 'But I happen to like nuisances. And if the day comes when I'm too busy to lunch a pretty girl, it'll also be the one I look round for a new job.'

It was too much. Karen got up from the table, taking her cup of coffee with her. She was drinking it in the kitchen when Ian joined her. He didn't say anything. He didn't have to. He just reproved in horrible silence. Ill-advisedly Karen rushed in to break it.

'I'm sorry.' That part was all right, it was the next bit that did the damage. 'Blame my queasy tum. I can't seem to swallow pap on an empty stomach.'

'Is that what you call it?'

'Have you a better name?' she thrust angrily.

'No.' His face was deadly serious, his eyes grave and considering.

'She's an infant who needs to be fed soft foods. But it's because of what she's been through.'

'She's not the only one to have known a nasty experience,' she countered, swallowing on tears, fighting to show the argumentative front, and, apparently, succeeding beyond her wildest hope.

'I know that.' Was he completely hoodwinked, because here the first hint of gentleness encroached his voice? It didn't stay, however; with calculated firmness he added: 'The ingredients might look the same, but they're not. Whatever the cover says, you and Val are contrasting characters. You should pity her, not condemn her for it, and be thankful your clash with fate made you a stronger person. Oh yes,' as Karen would have interrupted. 'That fragile appearance is deceptive. A man might think he can break you with one hand, not knowing he is in danger of breaking his hand in the attempt. In her case, it was Val who broke. The pieces were rushed to Highgate, a superior nursing home, all mod cons and resident psychiatrist. She reports back to him twice weekly out of necessity, and not because she can't bear the parting to be final. Actually she can't wait for that day, and neither can I. Do I make myself clear?'

'Crystal.' Did he practise making her look small, or was it a natural talent? And why, she wondered, did they always quarrel? Two more whys ejected in rapid succession. Why, in every argument, did he always have right on his side? And why couldn't she pander to the soft spot of sympathy his words evoked? Because, try as she might, she couldn't, couldn't be sweet and penitent. She couldn't even lose the battle by default, she had to put her meanness and nastiness into words. In her defence, it was the appeal in his eye that goaded her to say: 'I'll tie on the bib. But don't expect me to pick up the spoon and shover.'

She spent a miserable morning. There was no joy to be found in tidying and polishing the house, nor in setting to rights Ian's quarters over the garage, or shopping, or doing any of the things she had come to enjoy.

She lunched on cheese and an apple, she couldn't face more, and then got the sewing machine out from its new home in the sideboard cupboard. She selected one of the remnant pieces and cut out a nightie. If she couldn't be sweet, at least she could be decent.

When the phone rang, her thoughts automatically turned to Mitch. She didn't know why, except that he'd phoned her before. She didn't feel in a Mitch mood, and her hand very reluctantly went to the receiver.

'Hello,' she said, and it was as well she didn't anticipate the caller by name, because she was wrong.

'Karen?'

'Yes?'

Unexpectedly: 'Ian here.'

Her heart, equally unbelieving, gave a curious lurch. Perhaps he too had spent a miserable morning and was ringing to find out if they were still pals. Of course, she had a genius for being wrong, it was nothing of the sort. He'd forgotten, or the distasteful parting scene had driven it from his mind, to tell her it was Val's day to visit the psychiatrist. Her appointment was from seven till eight. He said he would deliver her to Highgate, hang around, and pick her up again at eight.

'So you want me to prepare a meal for say, eight-thirty?' presumed Karen, crisping her tone to match his.

'No, that's not it. I'm phoning to tell you not to prepare for us at all. We'll stop off in town. Get a bite. Make an evening of it. There's nothing to rush back for. Will you be all right?'

'I'll survive. Thank you for letting me know. Have a pleasant evening.'

She didn't know why she added that, unless she begrudged it them so much that she had to make amends.

I'll survive, she thought, when he'd rung off. I've survived lightning. I've survived a car crash. Surely I can survive an attack of plain old-fashioned jealousy.

CHAPTER NINE

'Okay, lady. This is a hold-up. Keep walking, or I'll let you have it.'

'Mitch. You idiot!' she said, without looking over her shoulder.

The finger in her back dropped. Three others joined it to lightly clasp her waist. 'Wrong approach?'

Wrong man, she thought.

'I meant it, the keep walking bit. There's a cafe not two streets away that does good coffee and mouth-watering Danish pastries. And don't say you can't spare the time, because I've been watching you dawdling aimlessly for the past few minutes.'

The barb went home. He'd phoned twice during the past three weeks and both times she'd made excuses not to see him. Not because she feared Ian's disapproval—that would have chased her into his arms—but because she had this thing about using people. It couldn't be a progressive relationship, and it didn't seem fair to lead him on.

'I wasn't dawdling aimlessly,' she disclaimed. 'I was deciding which belt to buy. I've narrowed the choice to two. A chic brown leather, or a snazzy gilt chain belt.'

'What's it to go with?'

'A cream dress.'

Is it pretty?'

'I think so.'

'Buy both. Ring the changes.'

She threw him an old-fashioned look. 'Have you ever had a money problem?'

He threw the look right back. 'Darling, I always have a money problem. I've got one at the moment.'

'Any expectations?'

'Such as?'

'A rich aunt pushing a hundred and two?'

'Er . . . no.'

'Then you're not worth cultivating.'

'I mean no rich aunt. I do have expectations. I'd like to tell you about them, if you've a couple of hours to spare.'

'I have,' she admitted, enjoying the repartee

and thinking perhaps she'd been over cautious. Mitch's sparkling blue eyes contained only light amusement. He didn't look in the least sex-starved; he wasn't hungering after anything she couldn't give him. 'It's Monday,' she added, basking in sweet relief.

His face went blank. 'Monday?'

She explained: 'Mondays and Thursdays my time is my own. Those are the days Val reports back to hospital.'

His mouth closed round an: 'Oh!' Like a horse thirsting to drink but balked by contaminated water, he got off to a slow start, drifting with his own strange thoughts, or whatever whitened his face, pulling himself together, smiling exultantly, rapidly catching up. 'In that case the cafe's had it, sweetie. My flat's just round the corner.'

'Your flat? Will I be safe?'

'As safe as you want to be, darling.'

She considered. 'Okay. Let's go.'

*   *   *

'Well, what's the verdict?'

'The cake is delicious,' she said. 'You must beg me the recipe.'

'I doubt if Cadbury's would give it. I meant the proposition.'

'Too daft to discuss.' She wiped her fingers on the paper serviette he had thoughtfully provided. 'Hare-brained. Ridiculous.'

'Well, thank you for the vote of confidence. Now would you care to explain what's so ridiculous about it.'

'The basic idea is all right.'

'Thank you.'

'I believe club turns are all the rage. You have talent. I recognized that when you played the piano, the night you took me to the Grapes. I guessed you were a pro. You fooled around, effortlessly, and made beautiful music. As you so rightly point out, the north is clubland. It's here, right on your doorstep. You say you have contacts. So go ahead. With the right partner you could make a go of it. But I'm not the right partner. It's me. Not you. I mean, can you see me as the crumpet half of a duo?'

'Seriously, yes. Otherwise I wouldn't have put it to you.'

'Then you must be blind, or something,' she said flatly, trying not to sound sour.

He considered before answering, taking his cue from the edge of bitterness in her voice. He supposed that just once every woman would like to be told she had ravishing features and a beautiful body, even if it was a blatant falsehood. Yet such flattery would insult her intelligence. And what did she mean by the 'or something'? He wasn't biased, if that's what she meant.

'I'm not blind . . . or anything,' he said guardedly. He wasn't in love with her, he didn't lust for her in the physical sense. On the other hand she did not repulse him. He dare not be too honest, because he was unsure of his ground. He hadn't yet decided which carrot would offer most enticement: himself, or the lolly. She might even be greedy and want both.

'Look,' he said, dropping the light approach and sounding splendidly earnest. 'I'll level with you. You haven't much of a voice, but it's adequate. You haven't—'

Her hand clapped over her mouth in quaking disbelief.

'You mean it! I do believe you mean it! Oh, do tell me it's a hoax? Tell me you're having me on?'

'No.'

'But I'm not beautiful or glamorous. I'm just not the image.'

'Right on two counts. Wrong on the third. You're the image I want. The 'in' image that's never really been out. Tiny girl, big stage to swamp you.'

'Where will you be?'

'Out of the spotlight, for the opening bars. It's just you and them, your audience. They look at you. And what do they see.'

'What do they see?'

'A green-eyed urchin, all set to creep into their hearts. The men'll reach out to protect you. The women'll adore you, because you aren't glam and don't have a beautiful body. You won't steam up their husbands and boy-friends. By comparison they'll feel glam and beautiful. Get it?'

'You have a vivid imagination.' She began to rock, she put her hands to her mouth and the laughter spilled round them.

He despaired: 'Why aren't you sweet and eighteen? You'd be easier to convince if the dew was still in your eye.'

He was serious. She was not. He couldn't make her see his point, she couldn't make him see how ludicrous the idea was.

'Oh, I'm sorry,' she said, reaching out and catching hold of his hand, feeling absurdly contrite. 'Truly sorry.'

His fingers bent round hers. Was that it? He would have to find out. His free hand went round her shoulder, drawing her close. Her eyes sent out green sparks of surprise. She didn't speak, she seemed incapacitated, but never had she been more eloquent, and he knew with a sinking certainty that she was not caught up in the Mitch net of charm.

Illogically, this angered him, and he forgot to tread warily. His hands slid over the body that failed to excite him, and his lips closed round the mouth parting to say his name. 'Damn you!' he said, his breath an angry hiss against her cheek. 'What are you made of?'

'And damn you!' she retaliated, white faced and choky. 'For thinking every girl will swoon at your feet. And double damn you for being despicable and dishonest. I asked. You said I'd be safe.'

'Not quite, darling,' he contradicted, his tone making a mockery of the endearment. 'I said, as safe as you wanted to be.'

'You thought that's what I wanted?' Her anger evaporated. She stared, twisting her hands, and when he didn't reply, repeated: 'You thought that's what I wanted?'

He tried to say yes, but muffed it. He felt downcast and ridiculous. But yes, he'd honestly thought that's what she wanted. For once in his life, he'd backed the wrong hunch.

'But you don't want me, any more than I want you. We haven't that sort of thing going.' She sounded incredulous and intensely shocked. 'Does it mean so much to you?'

He had to look at her. He didn't want to, but it was a compulsion. The mouth that he had so recently savaged, looked soft and tender. There wasn't a hint of derision in the expressive eyes. 'Yes, yes it does,' he was magnetised to admit.

She sat down on the sofa, patting the space beside her. 'I think you'd better tell me all about it.'

She couldn't be sure he did tell all. Because he lifted the lid to expose a layer of dark brown, it didn't mean there wasn't a layer of black lurking underneath.

'Mitch and Mandy was an established act,' he began. 'We did the clubs, got some worthwhile bookings.'

'Was Mandy your fiancée?'

'Yes.'

'What was she like?'

'Very much like you.'

'Is that why you picked me for the new Mandy?'

'Probably. I've got the contacts. If I don't change the act, or the name, it'll make it easier to get back.'

'What happened?'

'She couldn't stand the pace. It's hard graft. And she didn't like me being nice to the customers. Well, I mean, you have to be. There were lots of small unsavoury incidents, and one, concerning a club proprietor's wife, big incident. The breaking point came. It had to. We split up.'

'I thought you said she was dead?'

'Did I? I don't think so. We split up.'

'I must have misunderstood. Did you . . .' She hesitated, because of the delicacy of the question. 'Did you offer the ring because you loved her? Or as bait?'

His shoulders hunched, his hands slid through his knees to the floor. The ultimate in dejection. 'There are times,' he said, not looking up, 'when I don't much like myself. But,'—he thumped the floor like a madman—'Why didn't she know?'

'Know what?' probed Karen, swallowing to stem the full blast of her feelings. 'That she wasn't beautiful or voluptuous, or any of the

110

things you said she was? That all the time her mirror was right? You're a rat, Mitch.'

'I know, I know. I should have been destroyed, not her.'

'Is it too late?'

'I think so. The show is over . . . I guess. Like you, she wasn't interested in making fifty a week.'

'Fifty?' Her breath bucketed in her throat. 'Fifty what? For goodness' sake, not pounds? I'm not greedy, I don't want fifty a week. One straight fifty would do me.' There was in her voice a ring of galloping excitement and earthy realism. She was interested. She was interested!

His dissipation vanished. He was keen, alert, confident. 'Curse my perspicacious grandmother for letting me down. I placed the money last!'

She looked down her nose. 'Then you're a fool.'

'We'll practise. Work up a routine. We'll start with the little clubs and go on to the big ones.' Now they were both equally excited. He caught her to him and she hugged him back. And the embrace was light and superficial, as lacking in passion as the other had been fraught with it.

'My hat! This is it. I feel it.'

She clutched her throat, dropping from the heights to a sobering low.

'I won't wear itsy-bitsy costumes. I insist on

decent coverage. And I shan't tell Ian.'

'You shall have a hand in choosing your gear. But tell Ian,' shouted Mitch, all the way from his lofty mountain top of glory. 'Tell him to go to . . .'

'I can't. Not until I've made the first fifty. Anyway, he'd laugh. I can't bear to be laughed at.'

'Darling,' said Mitch, tossing her a peculiar look. 'He'd do more than laugh. He'd throw you out on your ear.' He was grinning and sniggering, as if he knew something she didn't. 'If he did throw you out, would it be so bad? You could move in with me. On a platonic basis, of course.'

'Thank you. But . . . no.' Marvellous how she kept her voice on an even keel.

'Okay . . . We'll rehearse here, in my flat, during the day. But if you're not going to tell him, you'll have to think up a decent cover story for when we start taking bookings. They won't be afternoon jobs.'

'I know, Mitch. I'll think up something when the time comes.' The trouble with Mitch was, he couldn't bear the thought of anybody not being ensnared. She must never let him know that she had resisted, not only him, but a flame quickening, a response to all that was evil in him, when he had brutally kissed her. She would never feel safe, when resistance was low, on a dark night . . . in a storm.

CHAPTER TEN

'I've changed my mind about Mitch. I don't like him,' she informed her troll doll. 'Not only do I not like him, I positively dislike him. He's working me to an early grave. I'm losing weight. And I can't afford to lose it.'

Mitch said the act was going well, after rehearsing for only two weeks. She tried to be infected by his fervour, but she felt unprofessional, raw. Perhaps because he was so polished and professional. He said the 'rawness' as she called it, was the quality she mustn't stamp out. 'It's what you're selling darling. You are raw. Cultivate it.' He said that before long they'd be ready to take bookings. One night stands. As breakers in. She panicked. She couldn't do it. What had possessed her to think she could?

She was also teased by another consideration. When the time came, how could she explain her absence to Ian. All right to say blithely, 'I'll think of something.' Another to think it. It wasn't as if she had a convenient friend to visit, or a relative.

Ian gave her housekeeping money, plus a wage. The latter he kept to a scrupulously fair amount, wisely knowing she wouldn't feel justified in accepting more. Not being what one would call a proficient housekeeper, she still felt grossly overpaid. He bullied her into writing to her father, to let him know she was well, and in employment.

Her father, who had never been known to keep other than a dry pen, did not write back. Angela did. She was reading the reply at the table she shared with Ian. Val was still upstairs, presumably putting on her morning face. Karen's own morning face was doleful, matching perfectly the heaviness of her heart. The letter, Angela's pen was not only well filled, but sprung with an amusing nib, did much to restore her spirits. She felt that at last her father had met his match. He should have tangled with her, years ago.

'Pleasant news?' enquired Ian, lifting his nose out of his letter, that had in turn come out of a buff coloured business envelope. Buff coloured envelopes never look pleasant.

'You could say, inspiring,' she answered sweetly. 'Angela wants me to get in touch with her parents. She thinks we should get to know one another. She suggests I pay them a visit.'

'Yes,' he agreed. 'You should get to know your stepmother's kin. Is she your stepmother yet?'

'Hang on a tick,' said Karen reading furiously. 'Not yet. Heck!' she exclaimed in dismay. 'You don't suppose it won't come off? I mean, why haven't they tied the knot? What are they waiting for?'

He had seen that same keen look of dismay,

once before on her face, when discussing her father's love. Then, as now, they had shared a table, but a strange table, and they had been so newly acquainted he hadn't known her name. It had rained hard, the day they met. In the bright, steamy atmosphere of the restaurant she had resembled a kitten, with misery drowned eyes. He remembered producing his handkerchief and wishing he could mop up the misery as well as the wet.

It amused him to remember she would have given anything to put the clock back, even Darling Ugly, the funny troll doll she was so much attached to, to a time before Angela. She had been progressively miserable because she thought her father was going to re-marry; now she was abjectly miserable because she thought he might not. Woman's prerogative, he supposed.

'Oh, it's all right,' she breathed, her relief heartfelt. 'It's further down. The wedding date, that is. It's fixed for October. I suppose that's something. She is hoping to come home before then. To do some trousseau shopping. If, and when, she will come to see me.'

'And give me the once over, I shouldn't wonder.'

She put her hand to her mouth, smothering an exclamation, and gasped:

'Do you suppose so?'

What is that meant to signify?' he enquired drily. 'Don't you think I'll pass the parental eye test?'

She giggled. 'Angela isn't old enough to have a parental eye. And I don't know.'

'You don't know! Well, that's very nice.' He pretended to look stern and dignified.

No, Ian, she thought, it's you who's nice, very nice. But the top layer, the face, dominated by the eyes, dark and satanic, coupled with the brutally bullying tongue, is all villain. Peel it away and you were smothered by the goodness of the man. If he bullied, he did so in your best interest. He made you face up to things that had to be faced up to. Like getting back behind the wheel of a car, to preserve your nerve. If he knew when to bully and prod, he also knew when to comfort and console. Like during a thunder storm.

In comparison, Mitch looked the bonny boy. With a blond forelock tumbling an unfurrowed brow, and bluer than blue eyes. Angels didn't come looking any better; yet underneath he was all that was bad and selfish.

'It's not always what the cover says, is it?' Her tone, thoughtful, yet seeking, coincided with his own deliberations. 'No, it isn't.'

'How do we know when the cover is wrong? What tells us?'

'Instinct?' he suggested.

'Yes, that's good. I like that. Mine's latent, only just coming to the fore. I'm changing my mind about people.'

'I had noticed.'

'And realizing it's better not to be too opinioned.'

'In the first instance, a less stubborn, more flexible viewpoint can save embarrassment,' he agreed.

'I wonder what Angela's parents are like,' she said conjecturally, thinking it wise to implant the notion firmly yet squirming because she hated laying bricks of subterfuge when the mood was so mellow. Yet she would need the cover when she and Mitch started playing the clubs, and it was too good an opportunity to pass up. 'You do think it's a good idea. For me to visit them?'

'A splendid idea. Only not this week. I don't like the thought of leaving Val on her own, not at the moment when she's showing such remarkable signs of improvement, and I have a business trip planned. It's overdue, I'm afraid, something I've put off too long. If I don't fly to Paris and haul out an export order, someone is going to haul me out.'

Val, Val, always Val. 'By the time you're forty,' she snapped irritably, 'you'll be completely grey and have a brow like a basset hound.'

'In that case I shall look very distinguished,' he returned, mystified. What had he said to cause such a large blot on such a beautifully peaceful cover?

He sighed, he tapped his foot, he looked at the clock. Val was taking longer than usual this morning. Karen's mind leaped again the ten or so years to his fortieth birthday. He would make an admirable husband; like most husbands he would gripe at being kept waiting, and, Val, who always had a last minute something to do—find a hankie, a book, that elusive glove—would certainly keep him waiting. But his patience would always find that last inch of stretch. And he would be faithful; his wife wouldn't need to fear the dangerous years, between forty-five and fifty-five, because he wouldn't swop one of her grey hairs for a dolly bird done up in fashion's latest.

His voice cut through her thoughts. 'Why so pensive?'

'I've just put twenty-five years on your back.'

'And that makes you pensive? Is it worse than the grey hair and the basset hound brow?'

'Much worse,' she said. 'Because I shan't be around to see.'

'And would you like to be?'

'Yes, very much.' It didn't occur to her to voice other than the truth.

'Then will you have dinner with me on my fifty-fifth birthday?'

'Thank you. I should love to have dinner with you on your fifty-fifth birthday.' It was a joke played out with serious eyes and grave faces.

'Dates of such long standing should be appropriately sealed,' he said. Taking her face

118

in his hands, he covered her mouth with his. She willed her lips to remain steady, even though she felt as if she was being slowly turned inside out. The suppressed feelings, the deeply buried urges, came to the surface, suppressing and burying that which had been a front, the unemotional facade the situation had forced her to adopt. Her mind cast out thought, she was incapable of logical reasoning. Her body, which had started off as taut as a bowstring, taut and determined, relaxed by degree. Relaxed, melted, trembled, finally acquiesced to the gentle liberties being taken.

'I'm sorry,' said Ian, looking troubled as well as grave. 'For that too-fierce embrace. If it's any consolation I intended only a light kiss, as befitted the occasion. It got out of hand.'

She wanted to say: 'It's all right, my darling. I'm not pressing bounds, or erecting barriers . . . it's all right.' But she was enthralled still, completely held in spell, and then it was too late. His eye was back on the clock, and he was saying:

'Would you mind going up and giving Val a knock. Officially she starts work fifteen minutes before I do, and if she doesn't get a move on, we're both going to be late.'

'Of course,' said Karen in hasty retreat, barely seeing the stairs for the tears stinging her eyes. She had, for a blissful moment, forgotten there was a girl with a prior claim, a girl with a fragile smile and an elusive quality, hard to define, yet more potent than obvious beauty. Obvious beauty is fierce and compelling, it is the sun with none of the subtle cunning of the sunset. The sunset doesn't blazon her charms, she doesn't put on a golden dress, dig her teeth into a man's skin, alternately burn him up with her brilliance, and dazzle him with her smile. Instead she beguiles and entrenches with a gentler radiance, which quietly and shyly keeps slipping from view. Everyone sees the sun, not everyone sees the sunset.

I can't even compete, she thought wretchedly. It's not the sun against the sunset. It's two sunsets, and mine happens to be the paler one, the unsubtle copy.

The trees were very near today, their heads, closely pressed together, seemed almost to enter the room. It was an illusion, of course, brought on by her fretful mood. The vista was the one she normally saw when dusting Val's room; today it only seemed touching close because the menace of something creeping and pressing matched her gloom and melancholy.

He was the faithful type. Perhaps if fate had been kind and allowed her to meet him first . . .

The dusting, the straightening, the general putting to rights, the wiping out the smudges and creases of yesterday, had ceased to be novel and had become as routine as a roller towel. Without a beginning, without an end, the job was never done. As soon as one smudge was obliterated, another took its place.

'Damnation to housework!' she said, venting her testiness on the empty room. 'I won't do any more today,' she vowed.

She made herself a cup of coffee and gulped it down. Which was stupid, she should have sipped it, to use up some time. A large chunk of morning lay heavily on her hands. Knitting, she thought, was strictly an evening pursuit. Rebelliously she picked up the needles and the ball of russet wool, and cast on. Within five minutes she decided she disliked knitting, disliked it intensely. Dressmaking she found enjoyable. Cutting out, the fascination of watching the scissors slide through the material, machine stitching, whizzing along the seams. A truly satisfying pastime, bringing instant reward. Perfectly suited to her impatient nature. With knitting the stitches had to be assembled side by side, then mounted one on top of the other, with soul destroying slowness.

Why doesn't Ian do something about Val? she thought. Marry the girl. Or at least come to an arrangement. Perhaps they had come to an arrangement. They might be lovers. No, no, no. She knew with a quickening certainty they weren't lovers, but the knowledge brought little satisfaction. Simply because she knew Ian wouldn't find any deep or lasting fulfilment in possession through strength. A man could so easily overcome a moral girl, with just the one priceless gift, that of tenderness. There isn't a woman on earth proof against tenderness. And the strong ones, who firmly believe they are made of steel, are more vulnerable than their frailer cousins. Steel can't crumple, it has to melt.

Karen knew she would just melt all over the place if she had to witness any touching pre-wedding preliminaries between Val and Ian.

She hated Mitch, but she needed him more than she hated him. Because it was his hand that would deliver her from this impossible situation.

CHAPTER ELEVEN

'Mitch, can you arrange a booking, quickly?' She wasn't being very sensible, she hadn't yet come to terms with what Mitch brushed off as nerves, but at least she was being practical. She needed the money, to pay off the debt, to be free of Ian.

Wouldn't it be easier, less of a strain, just to walk out? No, she'd been through it all, over and over again in her mind. She had to pay the money back first, then walk out.

'I wish you'd make up your mind,' said Mitch. 'First the deal's off. Then it's on, so much so that you want me to rush a booking, any booking. Be patient, sweet. I assure you, my want is as great as yours, but we must carefully select the right place for our début.'

'How patient?'

'I've a man to see tomorrow. I'd like him to see us do a number.'

'I haven't got a costume.'

'You have. I've been shopping.'

'You said I could choose.'

'Did I? Not to worry, I'm sure our choice would have coincided.'

'Where is it?'

'The changing room,' he waved a hand airily in the direction of the bedroom, 'is through there.'

The costume was laid on the bed. It consisted of a short skirt, with a full flare, in scarlet with a novelty diagonal overcheck in white. The blouse top was plain scarlet, with wide puffed sleeves, and a low scooped out neck.

She put it on. It made her legs look marvellous. She presented herself to Mitch.

'Very nice,' he said. 'But you've got it on back to front. It's supposed to be worn the other way round.'

She touched the scarlet material at her throat. 'I wear it this way, or I don't wear it at all.'

'All right, darling. Don't get touchy. I said you could have a choice and that's your choice. You look charming.' He caught her by the shoulders and propelled her round. 'You have lovely shoulder blades. Don't cover them up, just be careful not to stab me with them.' He walked round her until they were facing. 'Why do I get the feeling I daren't turn my back on you?'

It's not only a peculiarity of children to want what is denied them. If Karen hadn't shown her disinterest quite so forcibly, he wouldn't have given her a second glance. As it was . . .

She ignored both questions, the voiced one and the unvoiced one, and expressed a question of her own. 'How do I look?'

'Sweet and sixteen. The image is preserved. How do you feel?'

'Ridiculous. You've dolled me up to look like a cigarette girl.' She tugged at the wide sleeves, plucked the pelmet of skin. 'Only not as sexy.'

He chuckled. It was an un-beautiful sound. He went over to the piano, it was by the window, and aimlessly, lazily, with complete lack of absorption—or was it his talent that made it look effortless?—he touched the keyboard. Picking up his fingers, seemingly letting them drop where they wanted, as if they didn't belong to him, as if he wasn't personally responsible for the blissful, all the way to heaven, perfect, perfect sound.

'Come on, doll, to work. And for heaven's sake, look happy. Everything is just beginning.' But he was wrong. It wasn't the beginning, but the beginning of the end. She thought there wasn't a power on earth that would condemn her for feeling drained and miserable.

Work, even the incompatible variety, can be a solace. And Mitch, the working Mitch, had a special sort of magic about him.

'I don't know why you want me,' she said, when he'd called it a day, praised her feeble efforts, produced coffee. 'You'd do better on your own.'

'I tried going solo,' he said. 'It didn't work. To eat I had to take that crummy salesman's job. I might be the strength behind the act, but I need someone to draw strength from. Someone who looks tear-apart fragile, but isn't.'

'Me?' She flung out her arms, mocking him to cover up something tight and indefinable in her. A feeling, an ache, a desire . . .? 'Is it me you're describing?'

'Doesn't it fit in with your concept of you?'

'No.' That was it, it didn't. 'It fits in with the general notion, though,' she said irefully. 'Someday, when I suddenly crumple, somebody is going to get a shock.'

He went behind the piano to look out of the window. 'What do you know, it's raining,' he said. 'Look at the one legged mushrooms.'

She joined him to look down at the scatter

of moving umbrellas. 'There's a two-legged mushroom there.' A boy and girl shared the same umbrella. The girl's legs tapered into white boots. It was gentle rain, as soft as a blown veil. It jewelled the window boxes on the floor below, and glistened the pavement beneath the striding white boots.

'Val had a pair of boots like that,' mused Mitch. 'How is she, by the way?'

'Improving.'

'Is that a fact?'

'Ian's fact. I find it hard to tell.'

'What does she do? I mean, I know she sees a psychiatrist, but what does she do?'

'Writes things down in a notebook.'

'In God's name, what for?' He paled, looked peculiar. His expression went unnoticed. Karen was too busy staying her own pang of guilt.

'I don't know. I haven't been interested enough to find out.'

*   *   *

Ian said: 'My two girls will have to look after one another while I'm away. Don't forget to wash behind the ears and eat up all your protein.' Awkward glances were exchanged. He uttered a reflective:

'M-m,' then added: 'Oh well, I shall only be away for four days. Less if I can manage it. Then back to my piece of accessible heaven.'

'Is it still that?' said Karen, the more forceful Eve.

'Perhaps not,' he pondered, wondering why. His mind was taken up with other things, or he would have known why. The Garden of Eden had only one Eve.

Ian was away for three days. The days formed themselves into a pattern of housework, of rehearsing, of knitting (not much knitting, three days accomplished a paltry six inches), of watching television.

The notebook had a purple cover, spotted with white dots. It measured seven inches by nine inches. Two thirds way down the pattern of dots was broken by a parallel white bar, two inches in depth. 'Valerie Stainburn. Notes and Jottings' was written across this in violet ink.

Did its bright colour have a psychological significance? And what was the point of writing everything down? Ian had begun to tell her once, but she had not been sympathetic and he had dried up. Val said nothing. They shared a conversational vacuum. Did she find it easier to converse with Ian, or was this little book her sole means of communication?

If we can't communicate, we can't expurge ourselves of all the things that hurt us, and so they keep right on hurting us. That's what's called hell. Hell isn't a place, there's no down there. If we look down all we can see is our feet. There isn't any down. It's all up. We look up at the moon. If we stood on the moon it would be exactly the same. If we stood on the moon and looked down, all we would see is our own two feet. We'd have to look up to see the earth. Is that right? Can that be right?

No matter. Hell isn't a place. It's all the hurtful, painful things we lock inside of us. Hell is self-inflicted.

Perhaps I should get a little book. I would play safe and buy one with a green cover, just in case there is a psychological significance. Green is God's colour. If it has a significance it must be a good one, because He used it over and over again. Think of all the things He made green: trees, grass, the sea in a special light, my eyes.

I would write in my little book: There was a storm in the air. I could smell it. I could see it a long way off as a dark patch with splits of white. I wasn't afraid, by that I mean I had no sense of foreboding, or of terrible dread. It might fizzle away to nothing, like a cracker, fierce and sparkling and quickly spent. And even if it didn't, I wasn't unduly alarmed, even though I admit to a childish dislike of thunder storms, because, as I have been at pains to point out, it was a long way away, I hazarded a good half hour away, and my father was due home in considerably less time than that.

The table was laid. Señor don José Alvarez, who is very old and whose villa sits on rocks above a sparkling white arc of sand, brought the yellow roses that made such a delightful centre-piece. The señor is fascinating, his skin is like an almond shell, he is very gallant and often brings gifts. Not all are as acceptable as the roses. Once he brought sea urchins. He told me to split them open and eat them with lemon juice. I might have enjoyed the taste more if I hadn't known what I was eating.

I was admiring the roses and thinking about the sea urchins, and I didn't notice the spinning hands of the clock, or the fingers of darkness grasping the sky. It was very dark. Hot, still, waiting. I didn't like the waiting, yet I wanted the waiting to last for ever, because of a peculiar tight sensation in my breast. I experience that feeling even now, in bad thunder storms. I knew this was going to be a bad one. I don't know how I knew. I didn't think, 'This is going to be a bad thunder storm.' I felt it. I suppose I must have been having a premonition after all, because I felt it as a knife cutting downwards from my throat.

The thunder, when it came in giant rolls of sound, sound I could only liken to the sea, roughed up and magnified many times, was an anticlimax, a relief. Let what had to happen, happen. I couldn't live out my life in a vortex of waiting.

The lightning flicked the sky with a gentle whip at first. The clap of thunder had released the rain, it splashed down in fat drops, and the drops ran into one another to soak into the dry earth. The lightning was still a gentle whip making patterns, drawing circles and lines, filling the sky with a macabre beauty. I ran to the door to see if my father was anywhere in sight, definitely not to revel in the skyline.

It was an unfortunate impulse. As I looked, the lash tautened, and straightened into a point of descending white fire. It barely touched my skin, yet they said I was lucky to live, after being struck by lightning. They said not to worry, because the long jagged scar would eventually fade, and anyway, I could always wear a high necked dress. I couldn't take much of it in at the time. I became very hysterical. I cried out for my father.

When he came, he said he wouldn't leave me alone in a bad storm again. He didn't, not while I was under his roof, except in my nightmares. He didn't mean me to be alone then; I'm certain he would have crept into my nightmares, to cuddle and comfort me, if it was within his power. But it wasn't then, and it isn't now, and so I relive my nightmares alone. And I scream at him and shout at him, for leaving me alone.

There. If I had a little book, that is what I would write down, and I would be purged. But I haven't got a little book, and far from writing it out of my system, I've etched it more clearly in my thoughts. For a while longer I must endure my own inner hell.

CHAPTER TWELVE

It was an effort, but Karen did not turn back the cover of Val's purple notebook. It sat on her bedside table, in all its glossy splendour, as tempting as a grape. Begging to be devoured.

Karen picked it up, dusted beneath it, put it back. It fell from her grasp, falling open on the floor. She lifted it up, swiftly closing it to, but not before her eyes alighted on one letter. A capital M in the middle of a sentence.

M could stand for anything. It could be the M prefacing Monday, or Manchester. A word given a capital letter to mark a special significance. A name. Lots of names started with M.

All right, Mitch started with M. And it was her firm belief that if she dug to the root of Valerie's disorder, she would find a man. A man as evil and lascivious as Mitch.

No, she would not look in the notebook, even though it would explain all that was supposition. It was slightly more than that to suppose Valerie had tumbled out, not only facts, but thoughts that might be mad, pungent, or just nonsensically feminine. Thoughts that no other human eye should pillage.

Ian was back. Though technically he did not live in the house, coming in only for meals, it felt his absence as sorely as did the feminine usurpers. It was something less tangible than the ashtrays staying empty and cushions not looking as if they'd been in a rugger tackle, but a feeling that the pulse was taking a long pause. Then Ian was back, and with him the ambient sense of wellbeing.

'Any phone calls?' Without waiting for her reply he strode over to the telephone table, picked up and examined the pad. 'Ah! I see the butcher phoned. To tell you he was out of liver, but could do two nice pork chops. Also, Alice Newby phoned. Did you forget to pay for the newspapers?'

'No.' Karen's mouth fell open in perplexity and surprise. 'It was about a paper pattern I ordered for a dress. She was checking on the size. But how did you know? They were trivial calls. I didn't make notes.'

'Not notes, not in the recognized sense. But doodles. Did you know that every time you answer the phone you doodle?'

'No, I didn't. Thank you for telling me. I'll be on my guard.'

'Please don't. It makes a change from cross-word puzzles. And I'm getting quite expert at deciphering doodles.'

'Well, I'll still be on my guard. I might doodle something terribly indiscreet.'

'Or revealing.' His eyes held hers for a moment, searchingly. As if she didn't show much of what went on inside. Which was all to the good, considering.

'Where's Val?' she asked, sounding as brittle as glass, the way she always sounded when talking about Val.

'Visiting an old school friend. Kate Stevens. Apparently they bumped into one another at lunch time, and Kate invited her round to her flat for the evening. So it's grilled rump steak à deux.'

'It's pilchards on toast. You didn't give me enough warning.'

'How much warning do you want, to put on a pretty dress and—?'

'Is this an invitation to dine out?'

'What else.'

'That makes all the difference!'

When she was ready, she went into Val's room. The mirror in there was full length and she wanted to see herself in the cream dress. The material had handled well. The neckline, high, of course, gave the column of her throat a look of fragility. The bracelet length sleeves did the same for her wrists. Luckily she had spent her wages on a pair of strappy sandals. The purchase had left her insufficient money to buy even a hankie, but as she preened, taking in the effect of chic simplicity and long slender leg, she was glad she hadn't scrimped.

She never could enter this room without crossing to the window. It always had been, and always would be, the focal point, for her. The moon, which had given only a pinch-penny gleam of light for the last three days, shone as though it had been neonized. The trees clustered close to the house, protectively.

'Do I need a coat?' she asked Ian.

'No. If it's cold I'll lend you my arm.' It was a flirtatious remark said with neutral gravity. It was an assertion, an affirmation of what she already knew. Ian would always willingly lend an arm to someone incapacitated by a bad mood, or an unfortunate predicament. It occurred to Karen she'd had her share of both; she was determined the evening wasn't going to be rumpled by so much as a frown.

'Hungry?'

'Famished . . .'

'Those dancing sandals?'

She grinned and said positively: 'You bet they are!' She needed that hint of toughness about her if they were going to dance, make girl-man fun. They did have fun. When later, sometime just before dawn, he asked: 'Enjoyed yourself?' She leaned her head back against the door and said: 'Let me put it this corny old way. If good times could be boxed and kept, this is one evening I would keep for ever.'

'So good?'

'So good.'

'I'm glad.' He said that sincerely, neither under-emphasising, nor over-emphasising. The truth doesn't need gilding.

'Will you come in?'

His sharp: 'No,' raised her eyebrows. He

134

modified it to: 'Better not.' He picked her hand off the knob. 'It's too late to talk. And if I come in I might just forget myself. So,'—he gave her hand a gentle squeeze and let it drop—'goodnight. I'll see you tomorrow.'

'Tomorrow,' she repeated. It had a blissful ring to it. 'Oh! Not tomorrow.' Her voice sharpened, almost to recoil. 'I might not see you tomorrow. Of course, I'm not sure. The arrangement won't be properly finalised until I've had the phone call.'

'What phone call? What are you talking about?'

'Mrs Franks. Angela's mother. You remember me telling you Angela wanted me to get in touch with her parents. Well, we've . . . er . . . corresponded, and Mrs Franks is going to ring me tomorrow, to let me know if it's convenient and . . .' She realized she was saying too much, and her tongue was too agitated to be discussing something as innocuous as a social invitation. It was just that she'd been on edge ever since Mitch told her about the trio, scheduled to appear tomorrow, going sick. It was possible, just possible, they might be permitted to fill the gap.

'It'll be a wonderful break, darling. Bit more ambitious than I intended for a start, but . . .'

Ian was saying: 'Are you all right, Karen? Is there anything you want to tell me?'

'No, it's just that . . . it will mean cooking for yourselves, a bacon fry-up, or something. Or if

135

you'd prefer it, I could prepare a cold meal beforehand?'

'Anything. I don't look on you as a housekeeper, but a friend. A friend, Karen. I never meant you to tie yourself to the kitchen stove.'

'Oh well, that's all right then.' Her voice trailed off laconically, so he didn't need to rely on instinct to know something was wrong. Not with that wilting, turned-down mouth, and those rosier than normal cheeks.

He sighed. A woman's quick turn of mood was commonplace, not magical; all the same, he couldn't help but mourn the loss of his gay companion of the evening.

CHAPTER THIRTEEN

'It's on, sweetie, it's on. This evening Mitch and Mandy appear at the Seven of Clubs.'

Karen gripped the phone. 'Where's that when it's at home?'

'The other side of the Pennines, darling.'

'I can't, Mitch. I'm sorry, I'm ungrateful, I know what an awful lot of trouble you've gone to, but I can't.'

He bluffed: 'Of course you can.' He wheedled: 'You're not going to let an attack of nerves spoil the chance of a lifetime. Who knows, this time tomorrow you may be a star.'

'I know, Mitch. I didn't know before, but I do know now. I don't want to be a star. I don't know why I let you sweep me up on a dizzy cloud of make-believe.'

'Now listen to me,' he cut in. 'You didn't take much sweeping, you mercenary little—' He recalled whatever abuse trembled on his tongue, and suggested: 'Make yourself a strong cup of tea, and then lie down. When you're rested you'll feel better. I promise, what you're going through is not unusual. By this evening you'll feel fine.'

'But if I don't—?'

'You will, darling. Tell you what, I'll bribe some of the boys to come in extra early. We'll do a complete run through. You'll get used to the stage, the atmosphere, the feel of the lights. All that will be missing is the audience.'

She took an unsteady breath. 'Your grandmother's been working on you again. Because that is what I'm frightened of. I don't know why, but I'm frightened of the lights.'

'There's nothing to be frightened of. You'll be all right.'

'But if I'm not. If, when we've had a run through, I'm still not all right?'

'Then we'll call it off.'

'Is that a promise?'

'Yes.'

The tea helped. But she was too restless, too strung up to lie down. Anyway, there were things to do. House things, meal things. It all

137

helped. It wouldn't be too bad. Not with a run through.

But there was no run through. They got caught in a traffic snarl up, crawled the last five or so miles, and arrived at the Seven of Clubs with insufficient time.

'It's no good,' said Karen. 'Without the run through I can't do it.'

'You can.' Mitch hustled her up the stairs to her dressing room.

'You can.' His hand was on her elbow, whether his hold was captive, or merely to instil in her some of his strength, she did not know.

Her knees sagged, her jaw felt rigid. 'I'm sorry, Mitch. Call me everything you can lay your tongue to. I deserve it for letting you down.'

'You're not letting me down. I won't let you blast everything I've hoped for, dreamed of. Besides, if we don't go on, we get black listed. You can't do that to me. Quit tomorrow, if you like. That'll be okay. Tomorrow I can look round for another Mandy. But tonight you go on. Is that reasonable?'

'I hadn't looked at it from that angle. Would you get black listed?'

'I'd get sued.'

'You didn't mean it when you said that if I wasn't all right, we could call it off?'

'No.'

'Was the first Mandy this much trouble to

you?'

'Not quite.'

'But then, Val was in love with you, wasn't she?' Karen had no idea what made her say that, or even when she had assembled the idea that Valerie had been part of the act, that when Valerie broke up, the act broke up. It was a collation of conjecture and fact, a random surmise that was astonishingly accurate.

Mitch didn't say. 'That's a load of bunkum,' or, 'Val was never part of the act,' or any of the things she expected him to say. His jaw sagged, his face drained, he looked old and ill. He looked—this is almost impossible to believe—but he looked ugly. As if, all the time, his stunning good looks had been dependent on his cocky smile and his bursting self confidence.

And Karen overflowed with sympathy for him. It was unaccountable and unreasonable; he'd driven Val all the way to the black abyss, and had undoubtedly pushed her over, and yet she felt sorry for him. Probably because it was the first time she had seen a man break down and cry.

'Yes, she loved me. That's what I worked on to keep her going. Honest to God, I didn't know she wouldn't be able to stand the high pressure show business pace.'

'Was it that, do you think?' mused Karen, realizing he wasn't crying for Val, but for himself, for his shattered dreams, for his lost chance.

'Or was it the fact that she found out you had used her. That when the aces were down, you didn't love her at all?'

He didn't say anything. The tears continued to come, they slid down the furrows on either side of his mouth.

She buckled into him: 'For goodness' sake, man, take a hold of yourself. Do you realize we've less than fifteen minutes to change? And it takes me twenty just to put on my eyes!'

'Do you mean,'—he gulped—'you'll do it? After what you know, you'll still do it?'

'I'll try,' said Karen. Her voice broke and she said something peculiar. 'I can only hope it's the same thing.'

*   *   *

Mitch led her on to the darkened dais, squeezed her hand, then left her to take his place at the piano. The act had been announced, the clinking of glasses and the babble of voices had ceased. A hushed silence prevailed.

Karen could smell the roses on the nearby table. They were yellow roses. She had seen them just before the lights were extinguished. She tried to blank out the roses and think of something else during the few remaining seconds before the spotlight pinpointed her

140

aloneness. Something, or someone, to give her the strength she lacked.

Ian, she felt his presence as if he was nearby, but she couldn't see his face for the yellow roses. The roses out there were buds, the roses she saw were full-blown, spilling petals on the tablecloth. Giving them, Señor don José Alvarez had said: 'Poor roses. They have bowed their heads to a superior beauty.' She had smiled, because that is the way to receive a piropo. Like all his countrymen, the good señor was adept at paying extravagant compliments.

The seconds were running out. Mitch began to play the opening bars. The music rolled like waves of sound into her subconscious. Under her breath she repeated the words of the song, to make sure she hadn't forgotten them. An arpeggio sounded like a clap of thunder, now his syncopating fingers were making the tinkly sound of rain.

Karen could never be sure if she began to fall before the spotlight was turned on, or after. Perhaps it was simultaneous, because the audience saw the pale, petrified face in the descending point of white fire; then she crumpled to the floor, to lie like a broken doll in the wider, circular beam of light.

CHAPTER FOURTEEN

Ian ushered the manager and several hovering attendants, out of the manager's office. Karen occupied the only chair, so he sat on the edge of the desk.

'Start at the beginning,' he instructed, 'and tell me all about it.'

'Yes, well,' said Karen, accepting his presence with utter naturalness, although later, when her brain began to clear, she would marvel that her need of him had brought him so swiftly to her side. It had been Ian's arms that had lifted her off the floor and carried her out of range of all those staring eyes. 'Mitch said I had a passable voice and he asked me if I'd ever sung professionally. I hadn't, of course, and—'

'That isn't the beginning,' said Ian. 'That wasn't stage fright. I would say it was a collective effort. Correct me if I'm wrong, but I think ordinary stage nerves triggered off the memory of a bad experience. Begin there, with the bad experience.'

'Yes, I'll begin there. With the storm. You are quite right, it wasn't the stage or the audience. It was the blackness and the smell of the roses. It became very black, the day of the storm, and there was a bowl of roses on the table. Yellow roses, like those out there

142

tonight. They brought the memory very near. So that when Mitch began to play, it sounded like rain. I don't know if it did sound like rain, really, but the notes were tinkly and because my mind was keyed up to expect it, it sounded like rain. Then he played an arpeggio which sounded like thunder. No, I'm getting mixed up, the arpeggio came before the rain sound. Then the lightning struck.'

'I take it the lightning was the spotlight?'

'Yes, Ian. By that time my imagination was working full power because the spotlight stabbed, just as the lightning had.'

His grave face grew graver still as she described the burning sensation as the tip of white fire touched her skin. The simple act of talking about it pained her and all but stole her voice away. She was mentally and physically exhausted, but even so her fighting chin went up in a desperate bid to conquer this disabling fright-fatigue.

She put her free hand to her forehead. (Ian was holding her other hand, tightly, comfortingly, reassuringly.) Her forehead felt clammy and the room suddenly tilted. 'Drink,' coaxed Ian. She felt the thin rim of a glass against her mouth. Her lips slackened to let in a drop of the amber liquid.

'I'm better now, thank you. Am I having a reaction? I ask because I seem to be talking a lot. I want to talk and talk and talk. It's a compulsion.'

'Don't fight it. Talk is healing. It rids the system of a lot of poison. Talk as much as you want to.'

'Strange, but I can't think of anything to say now.'

'Say what is in your mind at this moment.'

'You won't like it?

'Say it anyway.'

'Well, I'm thinking about Mitch. I told you you wouldn't like it,' she said, noting the bunching of the muscles controlling his mouth. 'I know about him, by the way, what he did to Val. Not in detail. I know the skeleton of the story, not the flesh. I know her breakdown was the result of his treatment, plus her own vulnerability. Mitch is bad, I'm not saying he isn't. It's very bad to ride roughshod over somebody's ideals for purely selfish reasons. Mitch is very selfish, but I don't blame him solely for Val's condition. I think she was gulled by her own susceptibility, and you can't blame Mitch for that.'

'Why don't you say, even you? It's what you mean.'

'Perhaps. Do I sound to be reading the lesson?'

'Do you mean to?'

'Yes.' She didn't stop to consider whether she was being wise or unbelievably rash; she disregarded the whipping tightness of his mouth and the insidious drop, not more than a fraction of an inch, of eyelid, and ploughed

144

remorselessly on. 'I want you to rid yourself of some of that bitterness.'

In truth, he looked more surprised than enlightened, but he appeared to consider the possibility, though with misgivings. 'You're not suggesting I should regard him as a friend?'

'Oh no! That would be impossible. I merely want you to see both sides.'

'Why?' He forgot to pinch his mouth and looked—well, approachable. It clued her to say: 'Because,'—pause to swallow on a dry throat—'I think when you've stopped feeling sorry for me, you're going to be very angry with me. Not for going into this venture with Mitch. But for not telling you. I think you'll find the deceit harder to stomach than the action. I think I'm going to get a slap of that bitterness.'

He smiled at that, but still he looked mystified. 'Why did you, Karen? What did you hope to get out of it? Glamour? Fame? Does every little girl dream of taking the world by storm?'

'I don't know about every little girl. I can only speak for two. Val did it for love of a man. I hope it doesn't hurt too much to recall it, Ian, I don't know the extent of your involvement, but she adored Mitch. She closed her eyes and he dusted them with stars. She followed him blindly.'

'And the other little girl? You?'

'For love. Another sort of love,' she said,

rushing the words out as though glad to be rid of them. 'The love of money.'

'That surprises me. I wouldn't have thought you were mercenary.'

'I'm not. I needed the money for a specific purpose.'

'Why didn't you come to me?' he enquired in a light clement tone. 'I would have advanced you any amount within reason.'

She said awkwardly: 'I'm afraid you don't understand. I wanted the money for you. To pay back what I owed, so that I could go my own way.'

The smile left his mouth, yet the set of it was neither brooding, nor bitter, but gravely considering. 'Was that so very important to you, to go your own way?'

'Yes, yes, yes.' The words were torn out of her and she felt the sting of his tenderness under her eyelids. Because his tone was levelled with such a lot of patience and no condemnation, her fighting spirit began to wane; her thoughts were reduced to an economical low. 'I've gone through all that torture and accomplished nothing. And do you know who I feel sorriest of all for? I'm being stupid again, I know it, but I can't help it. I feel sorriest of all for Mitch.'

'You're wrong, Karen. I should say a great deal has been accomplished. As far as Mitch is concerned—' He went to the door and opened it, letting in, besides the draught that blew

146

down the long corridor, a vigorous, hearty, raucous, vibratory assault of sound.

'What is it?'

'Audience participation. The stuff they call applause.'

'You mean—?'

'Yes, it's for Mitch.'

She swallowed. 'With that much appreciation ringing in his ears, I see my sympathy is misplaced. How did it—?'

'Happen? Because he's Mitch. Because he's single-minded, his whole outlook is centred on the one purpose, it's called ambition; and because he has the gall to make capital of a situation that would have floored anyone but a true pro. And I suspect I'm tiring you,' he said, detecting the signs of strain and fatigue.

'Not really. In any case I shan't be able to relax, not properly, until my curiosity has been appeased.'

He thought over her words, digesting the element of wisdom; nodded, and continued: 'You folded up like a doll. I was still regaining my breath when Mitch got to his feet and shouted, 'If my playing does that to the little girl, let's see what it'll do for you.' It was fantastic, really, the way the audience was welded as one. You could feel the tension, hear the shocked gasps until Mitch stood up and said his piece, and then there wasn't a one among them who wasn't delighted to be conned. They loved it, they loved Mitch for

147

playing such a trick on them. You see, they believed it was part of the act because that is what they wanted to believe. Everyone craves a happy ending and well, after that ice-breaker—which, if I'm any judge will be a permanent feature of the act—Mitch couldn't put a finger wrong. He's made what is commonly known as a come-back.'

'I'm glad,' said Karen simply, ignoring the return of bitterness in his voice. He felt too deeply to rejoice for Mitch. As far as their own relationship went, she knew the evening had taken its toll. Although he had shown her nothing but kindness, he didn't for a moment hide the fact that he was displeased with her. How could he be anything else, hating Mitch the way he did? At one time she had hated Mitch almost as intensely, but not now. She felt only pity; it was almost as if he wasn't worth the greater emotion any more.

'I think I'm ready to go home, now,' she said.

On the first part of the homeward journey they hardly spoke. Although the situation had been discussed at length, she felt there was a small but important something that hadn't been touched on. A detail that eluded her. She went back, trying to resurrect the one thought, action, word that would activate the particular thought, action, word she was seeking.

It had been a funny evening, right from the word go. The dash and scramble to the club,

Mitch's tearful breakdown which had pushed her into something she hadn't been capable of handling. Ian's prompt appearance. Odd, how it had only just occurred to her how conveniently near to hand he had been.

Oh! She was remembering that she should have been at the Franks'.

'How did you find me?' she managed. Her dismay was acute and comic as she assimilated, digested, wavered between the two obvious courses.

'What shall I do? Attack? Pretend to be furious. After all, you didn't waste much time in following me. Or should I defend myself?'

Awarding her full marks for audacity, he said tartly: 'If the implication is that I didn't believe your cover story, that I deliberately snooped around, you should certainly look to your defence. You see, after you'd departed, supposedly to visit Angela's parents, Mrs Franks phoned you. To set up a meeting.'

'I see. That rather blew my alibi, didn't it? But,'—she hurriedly retrenched—'that doesn't explain how you found me.'

'Mitch did finalise the arrangement by telephone,' he pointed out acidly.

'Yes,' she agreed, latching on to his meaning. 'But you'd pre-warned me about my indiscreet habit of doodling. I destroyed the evidence.'

'Not exactly,' he corrected. 'I found it, after a search, screwed up in a tight little ball in the

149

fireplace. I'm only glad nobody felt cold enough to light a fire.'

'Nobody. Oh, you mean Val!' The tone of her voice was a mistake, and the tumult of her thoughts pushed her into deeper wrong. 'I wonder you could bear to leave her.' It was always the same when they spoke of Val. She put out a prickly antenna of dislike. Yet she would have sworn she didn't dislike her. It was just that she found it difficult to like her.

She put her back wearily on the seat, turning her face towards the window. Apparently engrossed in the ghostly shapes of the passing hedgerows. A bat flew out of the darkness, somewhere an owl hooted. Her heart felt like lead. No amount of chafing would dispel this new coldness that had crept between them.

'Don't take it out on Val,' he said through taut lips. 'If you think I shouldn't have meddled in your affairs, then come right out and say so. Or would that be too straightforward for your crooked little mind? You seem to prefer to dabble in deceit.' There was a long pause. He spent it regretting his harsh words because he said: 'I'm sorry. I shouldn't have said that. It was unpardonable of me.'

'It's all right,' she told him. 'If you remember I said you'd find the deceit the hardest of all to bear.'

'That wasn't the hardest,' he corrected. 'Oh,

I didn't like being lied to, but I appreciate your difficulty. You could hardly have told the truth.'

The car whispered over the bridge, down the twisty lane and through the stone gates and straight into the garage. They didn't speak again until he stopped the car, got out and came round to assist her. Then she said:

'I know it won't put things right. But I promise never to lie to you again.'

She fancied one eyebrow slid up as he said: 'So you're not planning to shoot off first thing in the morning?'

'No, I made a bargain with myself that I intend to keep. I won't leave until I've paid off my debt. Unless,'—hesitatingly—'you can't stand the sight of me any longer.' He gave her an eloquent look and said:

'You have some funny notions.'

'Will you come in for a cup of tea or coffee?' she enquired briskly, expecting him to say, 'No, I won't come in. It's too late.' Which is what he did say, but then he added: 'I'm in a talking mood and I might just waken Val.' Whereupon he placed a finger across her lips to prevent the usual acerbic come-back. But she wouldn't have this time because, incredibly, it certainly wasn't her doing, the mood had swung the other way and she wasn't going to let her quick tongue sour it. 'So why don't you come up to my room?' he invited.

'For a cup of coffee?'

'Or tea. Or to talk. Or not to talk.'

There are moments in life when everything is wrong, and moments when everything is right. The stars are crisper and brighter in the sky, so bright you think they can't possibly fade. But they do, reminded a tiny inner voice. Every star must fade for the coming dawn.

'I wish. I wish.'

'What do you wish?' he asked, taking her hand and leading the way up the steps at the side of the garage. 'I wish I could delay tomorrow.'

His quarters consisted of a bedroom and a tiny kitchenette. Karen threw off her coat and went to fill the kettle. It wasn't until she was standing at the cooker that she realized she was still wearing her Mandy get up. She wished she hadn't taken off her coat. She felt his eyes travel her low scooped out back and was conscious of how much of her tights the costume revealed.

'Was it strictly for the money?' he asked, as if that question tormented him.

'What else?'

'You're a woman. You should know the answer to that.'

'If you mean, was I in love with Mitch, the answer is no.'

'I didn't imagine you were in love with him. I thought—'

'What did you think?'

'Well, Mitch has a quality that draws the

152

opposite sex. An animal attraction. It's possible to want to make love to a person without being in love.'

'There wasn't anything like that. Anyway, it's over now. I give you my word I won't see him again.'

'I'm glad. Tea, or coffee?'

'Tea please.'

As he reached for the tea caddy, she reached for two cups. Their hands collided. Then they were in each other's arms. His hands were caressing her back, her neck, stroking her hair. His lips found the fluttering pulse at her temple, the hollow of her throat, her lips. Yet there wasn't a part of her mind or body that didn't react to the ecstasy of it. It was like being struck by lightning all over again, an encounter she would never forget, only the hundred per cent current flowing through their bodies was unbelievable delight. With touching egotism she felt that never before had two people been able to create such beautiful magic.

The spluttering of the kettle parted them. 'Do you want that tea?' She knew from his voice that he was as moved as she was. 'No . . . I . . . ought to go.'

He made a quick, urgent move towards her and she was electrified by the thought that he wasn't going to let her go. As a second wave of passion was released within her, she waited impatiently agog, wondering how she had survived all those years without him.

But his hands were doing a double quick retreat, and she was being bundled into her coat. 'If I can't see so much of you,' he said. 'I might just be able to let you go.'

She said through gritted teeth: 'You must be made of steel.'

The weight of his hands pressed down on her shoulders and she was being masterfully swivelled round to face the door. He whispered throatily into her hair: 'Think that if you like. Some day I'll prove to you that I'm not.'

He planted a kiss on the nape of her neck, for her to take with her, to cherish. Then he let her go with warming reluctance. As she sped across the paved yard she saw that the stars were beginning to fade. Soon it would be dawn.

CHAPTER FIFTEEN

Karen was cooking breakfast when Ian crept softly into the kitchen. He turned her round and kissed her full on the mouth. His glance, penetrating, with a light salting of mischief, raked her face. 'You look as if you positively enjoyed that.'

'I did,' she replied promptly, sheer astonishment crisping her tone. For some reason she'd thought the light of day would strip away the warmth and tenderness. She could still scarcely believe it had happened; that it was still intact was a source of throat-drying, speech-stealing delight. Only, she wished she could lose the lump in her throat and overcome this new, hampering shyness.

He was noticeably amused. 'I've never before known you to be short on words. You must be one of those people who are most articulate in anger.'

'And you would know all about that,' she retorted, her new-found voice wrapped round a chuckle. He said, with a good attempt at lightness:

'I've come to the conclusion we've been at loggerheads far too long. I'm glad I've found a means of disarming you.'

'Would you think me horribly forward if I asked to be disarmed some more?'

'I could never think you horribly anything. Damn!' he ejaculated, moving swiftly from the proximity of the cooker, but too late to avoid the spitting bacon fat. 'Why do we always have to make love in a kitchen?' he asked in amused exasperation, inspecting the angry red spots appearing on the back of his hand. Karen was looking meek and trying not to laugh, when she thought she saw a shadow flit away from the door.

The eavesdropper, if there had been one, could only be Val. How much had she seen and heard? How long had she been standing at the door? Karen fiercely resented the intrusion on what was a private and intimate moment, but that wasn't the reason for the icicle drip down her spine. Suddenly she was afraid. It was a stupid fear, a barely analysed feeling of disquiet. She told herself it was without foundation and in a moment her normal common sense would assert itself, telling her she was being fanciful and wrong. Until her composure was fully restored, she absorbed herself in examining his hand. 'What a fuss about nothing,' she clucked. A fuss about nothing. She hoped so.

'Will you be late home this evening?' she asked. 'It's Val's day at the hospital, isn't it?'

'Normally, yes,' he said, helping himself to the last piece of toast.

'But not today. Robert Williams, her psychiatrist, has gone on holiday for a fortnight, so rather than put her through the ordeal of getting used to a new man, she's having a break.

Karen looked at the empty plate. 'I'd better put some more toast on. What d'you suppose is keeping her this morning?'

'The pull of the bed, I shouldn't wonder. Didn't she tell you she was taking a few days off work? To catch up with herself, was how she put it. She must have found it pretty harrowing being plunged back into the working world. I'm not sure she wouldn't have been better off paddling in gently, but apparently it was for the best. Karen?' His eyes were speculative.

'M-m?'

'Try, won't you.' She knew what he meant, but before she had time to inch in her reply he began to elaborate. 'Remember what I said before about the ingredients looking the same, but you having a pound or two more starch in your make-up? What I'm getting at is, please make allowances. In a way you are both victims of circumstance. You lost your mother at an early age and so did she. She lost her father, too. You might curb your intolerance by remembering that you still have yours. She had only Grandmother and me. She was my grandmother's ward, by the way. Perhaps I haven't mentioned that.'

'No.'

'There's a lot of things I haven't mentioned, but with good reason. Before it was none of your business.'

'And now?'

His faint chuckle invaded the seriousness of the moment, making her feel less bleak, less as if she was hanging on some remote cliff top by the starch in her finger-tips. 'I should say recent events have made it your business.'

For a moment they enjoyed one another with their eyes, and with two thoughts pushing for prominence, Karen knew whichever way she jumped an opportunity was going to be lost. Selflessly she chose the one with the unpalatable taste. 'This must have been Val's home, then?' For the first time it came to her that she was the intruder, not Val. *I wonder she doesn't hate me.* But she does hate me, she thought with an involuntary flash of truth. *My feeling towards her is a reaction.* But Ian would never believe that. *He's known me such a short while and during that time I've done nothing to foster his trust, in fact I've done everything to destroy it.* She closed her eyes for a moment as a silent prayer trembled her body. *Please . . . please give me the time with which to build up that trust.* But she had the desolate feeling that nobody was listening.

'Yes, it was Val's home,' ruminated Ian. 'At first it was a holiday retreat. Then when her parents died she made it her permanent home. She lived here until Grandmother died.'

'You're going to be late for work,' said Karen, reluctant to end the discussion and so starve her curiosity, but feeling she should make some reference to the creeping hands of the clock. He was such a stickler for punctuality.

But he said: 'Then I shall have to be late, because there's something I must tell you. I have to return to Paris tomorrow, the deal I'm working on has run into unforeseen difficulties, so this might be the last opportunity for a day or so.'

She interrupted: 'You don't have to Ian.

158

What happened before we met is no concern of mine. It is that kind of confession, isn't it?' Suddenly she didn't want to know. She didn't know why, unless she was frightened to know.

He wasn't to be put off. With an unhappy laugh he began: 'At one time it was thought Val and I would marry. It wasn't anything as formal as an engagement, but more in the way of an understanding. Val's parents died in tragic circumstances; she'd only just begun to feel secure again, when Grandmother took ill. I don't think anyone ever had a more dedicated or devoted nurse. I could see she was wearing herself out, but she said it was her way of showing her love and gratitude for being given a home. She was so deeply shocked when Grandmother died, I thought she'd never pull round. Of course I comforted her. At first she was such a hurt little girl, then such a gay pal. I didn't for a minute think—' For the past few seconds he had spoken with his face in his hands. He looked up. 'I don't want to appear ungallant but she read a motive that wasn't there. And there was something else. Grandmother didn't leave a will and as next of kin I inherited the house. I've often wondered if Val had expectations in that direction. If she had inherited, I don't know what she would have done. There was very little money in Grandmother's estate and the house needed a lot spending on it in repairs, but in her grief she wouldn't see it as a liability.

159

I got all tangled up trying to explain it to her and she wrongly assumed I was asking her to marry me. I was deeply fond of her and for a while I thought it might be a way out.'

'It wouldn't have been. Fondness isn't a basis for marriage.'

'I knew that. What I didn't know was how to disentangle myself.'

'How did you?'

'I introduced her to Mitch.'

'And felt responsible for what eventually did happen?'

'That's about the size of it. I felt so responsible, I wished I'd married her and saved her from the whole horrible ordeal. I'm sorry, Karen, but that's the way I felt then.'

If I was a brave person, she thought, I would say, 'It doesn't matter how you felt then. That's over and done with.' Then I would challenge, 'What is important is how you feel now.' But I'm not a brave person. It mightn't draw the right answer. Sometimes not knowing is a lesser degree of hurt than knowing.

Ian had been gone half an hour when Val came down for breakfast. Karen didn't notice her strange mood because of her own preoccupation. Listlessly she watched Val attack the top of her egg with a spoon, smashing the smooth shell into tiny pieces. It irked her the way Val tackled her breakfast egg. She always sliced the top off hers cleanly with a knife. Pity I don't adopt the same policy with life, she thought wryly. Then she thought, measuring her distaste, if I'm intolerant over the tiny things, how can I hope for understanding over the major issues?

She went upstairs to do the beds. Val's first, pausing as always to look at the view, then her own. The Mandy costume was slung carelessly over the back of a chair. Last night she had been too tired to put it away. Too tired, too caught up in the ecstasy and wonder of being held in Ian's arms. Happy beyond belief. She'd always thought happiness was only in jeopardy when you took it for granted. She supposed that when happiness is yours for any length of time you cease to value it with the same intensity as when it is newly acquired. I wouldn't, she thought. I'd take it out every day and cherish it and keep it polished and shiny.

The longer you have happiness, the more able it is to withstand the knocks of life. A very new happiness is fragile, as fragile as an egg shell.

How will you do it, Val? she thought. Will you slice the top off my happiness in one fell swoop? Or will you tap at it and peel it off in tiny, messy little bits?

'What a pretty costume.' She hadn't heard Val enter her room and she was momentarily startled. Val prattled on: 'Is it for a party? A fancy dress party? I love parties, don't you? May I try on your party dress, please?'

Karen found she needed a few moments to

collect herself. Perhaps her silence was taken for assent because when she turned round, Val was falling out of her own muted candy-striped cotton and pulling the bright scarlet folds over her corn-yellow hair. She stood back for appraisal, her thumbs hooking her slight waist, long fingers covering each hip bone.

'Nice, m-m?' she solicited.

'Nice, m-m!' agreed Karen swallowing hard. More than nice. Val wore the dress in the orthodox way, so that the bright material brushed the nape of her neck and plunged to show the cleavage of her firm young breasts. Looking at the creamy perfection of her flesh, Karen felt a stab of jealousy because she could never wear the dress as it was meant to be worn, but must always cling to high necks because of her imperfection: her scar. Yet despite this difference, and the dissimilarity in their colouring, she felt as if she was looking at herself. She hadn't realized before how much of a type they were, even though Ian had frequently told her the ingredients were the same, she hadn't thought he meant it quite so literally. And yet, on the night, she couldn't have looked as winsome and as appealingly lovely as Val did at this moment, with her flushed cheeks and her long legs and a sparkle in her eye Karen couldn't remember seeing before.

Silly, but she wished Val would skip out of that dress and back into her own muted candy-stripe with the muted personality that went with it. There was something about this Val. She looked so gay and vital and alive.

An odd thought possessed Karen. She felt as if the clock had been turned back and she was being shown a glimpse of the girl she had once been, before she met Mitch and tragedy again overshadowed her life. The smile was no longer sad and quick-silver but assured, bubbling, free.

Karen didn't know when she began to feel afraid. Perhaps it was then; perhaps it was later when, for a moment, her eyes met Val's as she put the Mandy dress on a hanger in the wardrobe. For some reason the veiled, secretive look reminded her of the shadow flitting away from the doorway. In that moment she knew Val had witnessed that tender, private scene in the kitchen when Ian had pulled her into his arms. But if she had seen, what did it matter? She could think of no reason to observe secrecy, only this vague idea it would have been wiser in the long run.

As the day wore on, her fancies diminished. Val helped with the household chores, and her willingness and newfound gaiety infected Karen. She readily admitted there was a change in Val, but because the mood remained constant and didn't develop into sulks as she had feared, she not only accepted the change but owned to a feeling of relief. Still firmly convinced that Val had seen, she could only assume it didn't matter and she actually chided herself for having doubts. Everything was going to be all right!

In a little while she would start dinner preparations, she might even slip over and pack Ian's suitcase for his Paris trip tomorrow, to save him the task when he came home. Unselfish Ian, all cramped up in his room over the garage when he could be getting the full use of his lovely home.

Somewhere outside a blackbird was singing its heart out, and the sun skipped in at the window fingering Ian's desk and the solid oak gateleg table. She thought her father would like to paint this room. It was an artist's idyll, and a woman's joy.

She wondered how long the present situation could go on and wished she knew what the future held in store.

Val was sitting in the opposite deep leather armchair, her elbow punching a plump rainbow cushion. She sat up with an urgency of movement that sent the bright cushion spinning across the polished floor and galvanised Karen's attention. Yet nothing, nothing at all, could have prepared her for Val's bombshell as she said, straining slightly forward, her mouth teased up by the merest suspicion of a smile: 'Look, I know this is going to sound ridiculous, and if I could possibly rephrase I would. But do I know you?'

CHAPTER SIXTEEN

The blackbird was still singing its heart out in proximity to the window, which was open to billow the curtain, and the scents of an English country garden mingled with the fragrance of beeswax. Karen retrieved the cushion from the floor. It was the beeswax which gave it its lovely shine. Ian had told her his grandmother had used it to preserve and beautify, and one day when time rested heavily on her hands, she had set to with polishing rags and a vast reserve of energy and determination.

'What did you say?' she gasped, clutching the cushion to her breast as if it would ward off something that was ghastly and unbelievable.

'I asked,' repeated Val, hugging her slender knees and looking totally unconcerned, 'if I knew you. Do you live locally, I mean?'

'I live here,' she said, resolving to stay calm. Whatever happened she must not lose her head.

'Of course you do now,' said Val, her voice incorporating a chuckle.

'It just occurred to me you might come from hereabouts. Ian is such a stickler for drawing his labour-force from local inhabitants. Oh dear! does that sound terribly condescending. I didn't meant it to. Not when you've been such a brick and dropped whatever you were doing to come and chaperon me. Isn't that an old-fashioned word?' She wrinkled her nose. 'But then, this is an old-fashioned village. Perhaps Ian was right. Perhaps we should have got married straight away. Gran would have understood. She wouldn't have wanted us to mourn. But, I don't know, it didn't seem right. Do you think it would have been right, Miss—?'

'My name is Karen.'

'Of course, how remiss of me to forget.' She paused, to let the significance of her words sink in. 'But you haven't answered my question?'

'That's because I can't.'

'You think it's a matter for the heart to decide?'

What Karen felt like saying was, I think you're shamming. I'm ninety-nine per cent sure you're shamming. But she said: 'Why Val? Why are you doing this to me?'

'I don't know what you mean.' The eyes were guileless, yet Karen had to press on. 'Is it because of what you saw and heard this morning at the kitchen door? Or because I took your place in the act with Mitch?'

'Mitch?' queried the girl looking convincingly puzzled.

Karen's heart quailed. Desperately she said: 'Howard Mitchell. You must remember him.'

'Oh yes!' acknowledged Val brightly, and Karen began to breathe freely again until she added: 'Ian's always talking about him. He's promised to bring him home, one day soon, to introduce us.'

'No!' shrieked Karen, and before she could stop herself she leapt forward, grasped Val by the shoulders and shook her in sheer exasperation. 'You will tell me the truth. You will, d'you hear?'

'You're hurting me,' protested Val. Immediately Karen's hands dropped away, but the impression of her fingers remained on the white flesh. Val stared at the marks and a look of triumph leapt to her eye. 'You attacked me. I shall tell Ian and then he will send you away.'

'That's what you want, isn't it?' said Karen shakily, before fleeing from the room. Her legs were trembling so much she couldn't manage the stairs. She sat for a moment, hidden by the bend, and she heard Val lift up the telephone receiver and dial a number. It wasn't a miracle of deduction to assume she was telephoning Ian. What a tale she would have to tell, thought Karen, dragging herself up the stairs and out of earshot.

After a while she heard Val go into her own room. Karen went downstairs and busied herself preparing a meal while waiting for Ian to come home. She thought, the moment he comes in I shall know whose side he's on. But she didn't. She couldn't tell anything from his face. Apparently he could tell a lot from hers.

'Something's happened?' He covered the

167

distance between them in long urgent strides and took her cold hands in his. 'What is it, Karen?'

It didn't occur to her that he should have known what it was. She said: 'Val is pretending to have a memory lapse. She has gone back to the time shortly after your grandmother's death.'

'Are you sure?'

'That she is pretending, or that she has gone back in time? No matter, the answer is yes on both accounts. I lost my temper and tried to shake the truth out of her. But you'll know all about that.'

'How will I know?'

'Because Val phoned you. I heard her dial the number and begin to speak.'

'That's hardly conclusive. But we'll leave that for the moment. Why would Val pretend to have a memory lapse?'

'Because she eavesdropped on us this morning in the kitchen.'

'How do you know?'

'I saw her shadow flit away.'

'You didn't mention it.'

She shrugged her shoulders. 'I didn't think it was important.' He pondered for a moment. 'Why didn't I see anything?'

'Because the bacon fat splashed on your hand and that occupied your attention. But why are you asking me all these questions?' she said pulling her hands out of his. He didn't reply straight away, and then he harked back to an old theme. 'You don't like Val very much, do you?'

She gasped: 'That's got nothing to do with it. Are you suggesting I'm inventing it?'

'That isn't the word I'd choose. Val didn't telephone me,' he said levelly. 'This is the first I've heard of it.'

'Then who did she phone?' puzzled Karen in dismay. 'What further mischief is she plotting?'

He said tonelessly: 'Is she in her room? I'll go up and have a word with her.'

When he came back down, a good twenty minutes later, he said: 'I admit she seems unwilling to talk about things, but I'd say it's a natural reluctance, not a memory lapse.'

Karen stared in stricken disbelief. It was a full minute before she thought to urge: 'Phone the hospital. They'd know. They'd see through her straight away.'

He said, giving his words a good deal of thought: 'If there's anything to see through. Would you ask me to put her through the whole harrowing ordeal again, on a mere hunch?' When he saw how unhappy she looked he added: 'I might at that, but the one who knows her inside out is on holiday.'

'Damn! I'd forgotten that. Will you still go to Paris?'

'Sweetheart.' His arms reached out to her and held her in a bear hug.

'Of course I must go to Paris. Admit you could have done some conclusion jumping about the eavesdropping . . . and the phone call.'

She opened her mouth to protest, then remembered she had jumped to a conclusion about the telephone call. 'Please Ian, don't go to Paris. Call it a hunch or what you like, but I know something is going to happen to drive us apart if you go to Paris tomorrow.'

He frowned. 'I must go. But if it will please you, I'll telescope three days' work into one and catch the first available flight back. I'll even book a telephone call for tomorrow evening at nine-o'clock to make certain you're all right.' With that Karen had to be satisfied.

Next morning Val seemed perfectly recovered, and Karen wondered uneasily if she could have imagined it. Then she thought crossly, of course I didn't. All the time she watched Val, trying to gauge what was going on in her mind. Twice she caught her laughing surreptitiously and this increased the agony of waiting. Finally, when she thought she could bear the suspense no longer, Val said she was going out for the day.

'I'd rather you didn't,' said Karen.

That met with a puckish smile. 'Because of my memory lapse? We both know I invented that.'

Mystified Karen asked: 'Why? It doesn't make sense.'

'Have patience,' said Val. 'It will.'

'I don't know what you are going to do, or why you are going to do it,' said Karen wearily. 'You can't want Ian. You don't love him.'

Val walked over to the window and stared at the trees. 'I hate this view,' she said aggressively. 'I wish the Forestry Commission would chop the trees down. No, I don't love Ian. But I still want him. He makes me feel cherished and protected.'

'That's not enough, Val.'

'It is for me. I've known love, remember. It swallows you whole, like the trees out there. Perhaps you like being swallowed whole?'

'Perhaps I do at that. I like going for walks in the wood. I want Ian to love me. Please don't spoil it for me.'

In replying, Val touched on a tender spot. 'How do you know there's anything to spoil? Can you say he loves you on the strength of a kiss or two?'

'No.' In his own words, it's possible to want to make love to a person without being in love with them. He'd said that just before taking her in his arms.

'Ian hates Mitch,' said Val. 'He wasn't very pleased with you for teaming up with him.'

'He told you about that?'

'Everything.'

That's a fabrication, thought Karen. He didn't tell you. I can sense you know all about it, so somebody must have told you. But not

171

Ian. But there's no other interested party, save for perhaps, Mitch.

'Doesn't it scare you what would happen if you repeated the indiscretion?' probed Val silkily.

'Not really. Because I've no intention of getting involved with Mitch again.'

'How definite you sound,' mocked Val. 'Let's hope your determination doesn't come unstuck.' The undertone of a threat made Karen's finger-tips curl, and she was glad when Val did go out. 'Don't expect me back much before breakfast time,' she called out. Karen didn't know if she meant it or not; moreover she was beyond caring.

After that time dragged interminably. Karen kept looking at the clock, willing the hands to rush to nine, which was the time Ian had promised to phone her from Paris. Perhaps when she heard his voice she would feel comforted, more secure.

It was still only ten minutes to six. To make the time pass more quickly she decided to take a short walk. Hurriedly she changed her dress, as she was closing the wardrobe door, she realized the Mandy costume was missing. She looked again to make certain, and then checked the contents of her drawers although she was reasonably certain she had hung it in the wardrobe. Was Val a thief as well as an eavesdropper, because of course she was the only person who could have taken it? And what would she want with it?

It gave her something else to puzzle over as she plunged down her favourite woodland path. Above the towering pines, jagged chinks of blue indicated it was still day. Tiny feathered bodies flittered between the spiky green branches and entertained her with a song as sweet as a choir of angels, punctuated now and then by the screeching call of a jay. A red squirrel looked at her for a moment with bright, inquiring eyes, before streaking up a tree and out of sight, his bushy tail catching fire in the westering rays of the sun.

She skirted a path fairly near the edge of the wood, as the paths all looked notoriously alike and she had no wish to get lost and risk missing Ian's phone call. She was filled with peace and tranquillity, her problems shrunk to perspective; when she spoke to Ian her voice wouldn't have an edge to it. She hazarded she had walked far enough, time to turn back.

She didn't know quite how it happened, one moment she was swinging along with free, easy strides, and the next her foot hooked itself round the root of a tree and she lay winded on the ground. As she moved, a pain stabbed her ankle and she had a horrible vision of having to limp slowly back, and thought what a good job it was she had plenty of time.

Then she saw it, something white and still tucked in the undergrowth. If she hadn't fallen she wouldn't have spotted it. With gentle hands she lifted it out. It was the prettiest mallard, glistening white with patches of velvety black.

'What are you doing here, you beautiful boy?' she whispered, searching her mind for explanation. Overhead, telegraph wires were partially hidden by the trees. It seemed likely that in the failing light he had flown into them. Luckily the undergrowth had broken his fall. Holding him she felt the flutter of his heart and knew he was only stunned, but the pose of utter helplessness filled her with quick compassion.

'You poor thing,' she murmured softly. Perhaps not so helpless at that because he cocked open one eye and gave her a saucy look as if to say: I'm all right now. You'll look after me.

'I will. I will,' she said. Unmindful of her aching ankle, she began the long trek down to the river, carrying her warm bundle. Once or twice the duck jerked convulsively, as if he was in pain. He seemed to know he was in caring hands because he gave her a trusting look before firmly closing his eyes. She decided to make a detour by way of St Mary's Church. The vicar was usually pottering about at this time of day, and with his knowledge of wildlife he would know if the duck was really hurt. Because she knew she couldn't abandon him until she was certain he could fend for himself.

But as she approached the strip of bank

proceeding the church, the duck decided he'd been passive long enough. His head went back, his bill opened, and with a series of squawks he spread his wings and took off, keeling her over in surprise. Yet delighting her with the picture he made as he circled twice before sweeping off into the sunset. She watched until he was a speck against a skyline speared with gold, orange and red.

Still she did not move. The clock in the church tower began to strike. She counted, one, two, three. It couldn't be all that late. Four, five, six. And yet she had the feeling her worst fear was about to be confirmed. Seven, eight, she couldn't have missed Ian's telephone call, she couldn't. But as the ninth chivvying stroke sounded, she knew that she had.

She came very near to sinking down on the ground and weeping tears of frustration. To wait all day for this moment and then let it slip through her fingers. Her first big mistake had been in caring for the duck. But she hadn't known it would come to no harm. In any case the damage was done and all the crying in the world wouldn't put the clock back.

She thought, as she plodded a few weary paces on an ankle that was beginning to puff up and had started to ache abominably, that she spent too large a proportion of her life moaning about the inflexibility of time.

Her ankle was paining her so badly, she wondered if she would make it home and actually toyed with the idea of retracing her steps and slipping into the church to rest for a while. Perhaps the vicar would take pity on her and drive her home. Ah, the vicar! She'd met him on several occasions and found him to be a jovial type with a keen, one might say dedicated, interest in his fellow man. He would want to talk, which was bad enough as she didn't feel in the mood for polite chit-chat. But worse, she knew her face wasn't a study in tranquillity; she was nervy and on edge again, and being the kindly soul he was he'd want to know why. She couldn't tell him why because she didn't know the answer to that herself, and she couldn't fob him off with vague untruths. Not the vicar, that would be too irreverent. She decided to brave it home as best she could, which was her second big mistake of the day. If she had turned back to the church the vicar would have been in a position to provide her with an alibi. But then, she didn't know she might be called upon to account for her time.

CHAPTER SEVENTEEN

Next morning she woke to the fact that she'd slept, although she had thought she wouldn't with so many problems tearing at her mind, and that her ankle was in good fettle. The swelling had subsided and, gingerly she put it

176

out of bed to test it, it seemed able to take her weight. Well, that was something anyway. Whatever fate Val was plotting she wanted to meet it standing squarely on her own two feet. Val was up to something but, although she lay awake into the small hours, she hadn't been able to fathom what it could be.

In truth she hadn't lain awake solely on Val's account. She had hoped when Ian got no reply, he might book a later call, but it had been a forlorn wish and she hadn't been too surprised when the phone remained silent. She heard Val come in around one-thirty, and sometime after that she must have dropped off because when she opened her eyes it was morning.

Sometime between breakfast and lunch, the Mandy dress was returned to her wardrobe. Puzzling, she conceded, but surely not significant. The truth, the horrible, unbelievable truth did not catch up with her until late in the afternoon.

Yet afterwards she wondered if she could have had a premonition, without knowing about it, to account for her strange mood. For example, she wanted to cling to the poignant beauty of the day, wanted to imprint on her heart every aspect of the view, as if tomorrow it might not be there. As if it could suddenly be transported.

The sun glinted in and out of the trees and the fell had never looked as majestic in its gold and purple cloak. She wondered what it would look like in the depth of winter, crusted in white, the trees brushed with silvery splendour, glittering like the enchanted forest of a fairy tale. She ached to be able to see it in its winter dress and its spring dress. She wanted to see it for all the seasons to come, but she couldn't see how that could possibly be. The house had suddenly become too small for both her and Val. Ian would have to choose, but she daren't for the life of her dwell overlong on that thought, let alone pursue it.

Her daydreaming had thrown out her daily schedule, so she was late setting out for the shops. Val delayed her further by showing a sudden eagerness to talk. She had been out for the better part of the morning and by tacit consent they'd eaten lunch in wary silence.

Karen was torn in two. She wanted to stay and hear what Val had to say, but ostrich-like she wanted to defer any unpleasantness. In the end curiosity won and she stayed.

'Did Ian say what time he'd be back?' Val murmured interrogatively.

'Not exactly,' said Karen. 'He mentioned something about booking an earlier flight. I meant to ask him if he'd had any luck when he phoned yesterday.'

Val's supercilious smile was swallowed by a look of surprise and mortification. 'What time did he phone?'

'Nine o'clock.' Foolish honesty made Karen

178

add: 'But I didn't speak to him. I wasn't in to take the call.'

Relief sprang to Val's eye. 'How thoughtful of you to tell me,' she simpered, twisting a strand of hair round her finger and epitomising girlish sweetness. So that it came to Karen's mind, no wonder Ian is fooled because when she looks like that I can wonder if I'm doing her an injustice. Is she capable of deep cunning? It was hard to discriminate between that and what could be a childish desire to draw attention to herself. As if for a moment Ian wasn't aware of her plight.

Karen called at the butcher's first. Willie Smith was a dapper little man, always affable and polite. She thought he looked out of place in his blue and white smock, he would have made a splendid jockey or a dancer. But horseflesh would certainly be out of bounds in this shop, and his dancing activity was curtailed to a quick-step round the chopping block.

'And what's it to be today? The lamb chops look nice.'

'Steak, please,' said Karen. 'Fillet if you've got it.'

'I think I can accommodate you.' He was swinging open the fridge door and disappearing inside. 'Didn't know you did the clubs,' his voice floated out to her. It made her smile to think the news of her debut at the Seven of Clubs had travelled over the

Pennines, all the way to Hamblewick.

'I don't,' she said. 'My first attempt proved to be a disastrous effort which I will never again repeat.'

'Oh?' He returned balancing the meat on a piece of greaseproof paper and slapped it on the scales. 'So it wasn't a publicity stunt like they're all saying? You really did come over faint?'

'I did. Do you think I'll ever live it down?'

His eyes twinkled. 'No.' The steak was wrapped and duly paid for.

In the next shop she met the curious and disapproving—though why disapproving?— eyes of Pat Dawlish, as she came out of her post office cage to flit behind the grocery counter. 'Fully recovered, I trust?'

'Recovered?'

'From your ordeal of yesterday evening.'

'Oh you mean with the duck.' She blushed to think someone had spotted her limping gamely down to the river's edge. What an idiot she must have looked, especially when the bird suddenly took off. A picture of herself clutching the duck floated before her eyes, melting her embarrassment as she saw the funny side of it.

'Not with, at,' said Pat Dawlish, grim mouthed. 'And not the Duck, but the Cat's Whisker.'

Karen sobered instantly, to stare and digest the words, and tie them up with Willie the butcher's words and make them into a horrible sense. Obviously he hadn't been referring to her appearance at the Seven of Clubs three days ago, but to a happening as recent as yesterday, not across the Pennines but much nearer home.

'The Cat's Whisker?' she said on a cautionary note, wanting to be certain it was the truth she had latched on to. 'Mitch and I appeared at the Cat's Whisker last night? At Todbridge?' Please not there, practically on the doorstep. But, yes that one as Pat confirmed with a crisp nod before asking: 'Are you all right?'

'Yes, it's just that there seems to have been a mistake,' she said miserably as she bolted out of the shop.

'Your picture's in the Hamblewick and District News,' Pat Dawlish called after her. 'It's not a very good likeness. But then, you can only see a bit of your back.'

That figures, thought Karen wretchedly. Val would see she didn't face the camera, because of course it was Val. The time she had suspected her of phoning Ian, she had been phoning Mitch and hatching up her plot. It all fitted, her smugness, her reason for borrowing the Mandy dress, even her stricken look when she believed Ian had spoken with her on the telephone at nine o'clock. Which time presumably coincided with her appearance on stage. A fleeting appearance according to the evidence of Willie.

Damn! Damn! Damn! Well, anyway, her frustration wouldn't be aggravated for long. Ian was bound to find out as soon as he put a foot in Hamblewick. Pat Dawlish would inform him for certain. If he arrived back today, which was more than a possibility, he would see for himself because it was his custom to stop off at the newsagent's to collect the local evening paper. Then she would have the unenviable task of explaining she hadn't gone back on her promise to have nothing more to do with Mitch, and all the time it was Val.

He would give her a cynical look and say: 'Oh?' in that disbelieving way of his. Or worse he'd put on his long-suffering face and say: 'The trouble is, you have never liked Val.' Even so he must see that it was feasible, because who could impersonate her better than the original Mandy: Val. So then he would trot her round to see Mitch for confirmation of her story. Mitch might well have been a party to Val's deception, it would delight his perverse sense of humour, but he wouldn't lie when it came to a show-down. That was the puzzling part. Why had Val done it, when she couldn't hope to get away with it?

Karen stopped dead in her tracks, knowing why. That way would be too degrading. She wasn't a sack of potatoes to be hauled here and there, nor an untrustworthy child whose word is to be doubted. She had to say, "It

182

wasn't me." And if he loved her, he had to believe her because that is what love is all about, trusting a person, believing them implicitly when the facts state otherwise.

'That isn't me,' she said stabbing the photograph in the Hamblewick & District News.'

'I know,' said Ian.

'Just this once the indisputable facts are . . . what did you say?'

'I said I know it isn't you.'

Her anxiety switched off and she stared at him, numb with relief. 'You know!' For one heady, glorious moment she gloated in silent wonder, before an intrepid desire for confirmation goaded her into saying: 'You trust me . . . implicitly?'

'Trust doesn't come into it,' he said, wriggling uncomfortably.

'What do you mean?' Her joy was momentarily blighted.

'Just what I said.' He avoided her shrewd eyes, rubbed his chin, and challenged: 'Have you looked at the picture?'

'Yes,' she replied shortly.

'I don't think you have.' He was still looking anywhere but at her. Puzzled, she reached for the paper to examine it critically. It was a marvellous shot of Mitch, his face looked splendidly handsome in semi profile. Not so good of the girl. Val showed the camera her back. People's backs tend to look much alike

183

and she couldn't see . . . 'Oh!'

'Precisely,' he said as the tell-tale colour rushed to her cheeks.

'Your dress, but not your back. That back is covered, which means the girl's front must be . . . uncovered.'

'The word is décolleté,' she submitted miserably.

'And you wouldn't wear a dress with a décolleté neckline, would you?'

'No,' she said, embarrassment hollowing out her voice, yet she wasn't so totally submerged that she couldn't acknowledge the demon of amusement enjoying the fact that it was a bit of a suck in for Val. Val had slipped up badly in her impersonation, but then she didn't know Karen wore the dress back to front, for a very special reason. He wasn't supposed to know, either. When she told him about the lightning, she hadn't been able to bring herself to mention the extent of that.

His hand cupped her chin, then dropped boldly to outline her scar.

'Not such a terrible disfigurement,' he said meaningly. His voice, as gentle as his touch, stirred her heart. 'You can't . . . know?'

'I can,' he said kindly. 'Let's say I found out sooner than later.'

'How much sooner?'

'The first night you came here you had a nightmare. I rushed in like Galahad to find m'lady skimpily attired!

184

She swallowed. 'It's a relief actually, that you know and don't . . .' Her voice fell into unhappy silence.

'Finish what you were going to say,' he commanded, his expression softening to give her the confidence she lacked.

'Find my body repulsive?' she croaked.

'My darling, I could never find you that. Beautiful, adorable, very, very desirable. Never, never repulsive. Please don't cry.'

'I'm sorry, but I always cry when somebody tells me they find me desirable.'

'Have there been many?'

She giggled weakly, because he asked this so tentatively, then she rushed to assure him: 'You're the first. I'm making such a fool of myself. But you see, I didn't know.'

'Didn't know that I love you and desire you to distraction? But you must know. Why else would I ask you to marry me?'

'But you haven't,' she protested.

'Nonsense! Of course I have. I asked you to dine with me on my fifty-fifth birthday.' Denuded of argument by the memory of that occasion, she could only weakly gasp: 'And that was a proposal?'

He contrived to look hurt. 'What else! You'll surely be married by then, you're not spinster material. I hope you don't think I'd take out another man's wife. That would make me a lecherous old so and so.'

'Oh, Ian!' she said, sliding her hands up and

round his neck. 'That is a proposal. A beautiful proposal. Did I accept?'

'Of course. Now, may I ask where my fiancée was when I phoned yesterday evening?'

'Your fiancée? Oh! you mean me! Darling, I can explain but,'—she broke off to giggle—'it is a bit of a lame duck tale. So do you think it can wait because I want you to kiss me so desperately.'

She was already in his arms. All he had to do was bend his head. His mouth was half way to hers when his body stiffened and drew back. She didn't look round. She waited a moment and then heard him say:

'Hello, Val.'

'Ian, you're back!' She slunk into the room like a guilty child who knows she has been naughty and awaits punishment. Karen felt nothing but admiration for Ian as he squeezed her hand, intimating, 'We'll carry on where we left off, later' before going over to Val. 'Sorry love,' he said. 'It didn't work. Like to tell me why you did it?'

For a moment she looked as if she would deny all knowledge. Then, wearily shrugging her shoulders she said: 'I wanted to discredit her,'—indicating Karen with a haughty thrust of the head—'in your eyes.'

'Why did you, Val?' he asked so patiently that Karen felt a rush of gratitude because he loved her, wanted her . . .

'Because I didn't want to lose you.'

. . . and compassion because Val hadn't been as lucky in love. Before Ian could voice an answer, she rushed in impulsively: 'You won't, Val. We're your friends. Both of us.'

The telephone was ringing. Ian is calling from Paris, thought Karen, struggling through the hampering layers of happy somnolence. I'm not too late after all. But I must hurry, hurry, before he rings off. Because I'm not answering he might think I'm not here. Wait Ian, please my darling, wait for me. I'm hurrying, only I'm not making progress. I can't . . . walk very well, my throat hurts and my eyes are stinging so much I can't see.

My eyes are open now. I'm awake. I'm realizing it isn't then, but now. That isn't Ian on the telephone because he's not in Paris, but asleep, probably, in his room over the garage. I still can't see. I'm on the stairs. I know I'm on the stairs because I'm feeling the steps with my hands, but I can't see for the black, thickening smoke.

Oh, my God! The house is on fire! Val, where is Val? In her room? Is she sleeping through this or is she, perhaps, overcome by the fumes?

She turned to fight a way through the dense blackness until she was standing in the long corridor outside Val's room. Terrifying sounds came from within. Fierce crackling noises mingled with the ferocious whine of the wind,

187

but she hesitated for only a brief moment before fumbling for the knob.

Instead of the blazing inferno she half dreaded: more smoke, if possible thicker and denser. She groped her way to the window, to stop in horrified fascination. The forest, her beloved forest, resembled a series of lit torches. The heat was unbearable, even as she watched the pane cracked, sounding like the report from a gun, showering her with fragments of glass. Painfully she backed away; coughing, spluttering, she found the bed, punching its emptiness before retreating, hoping, as she progressed slowly down the stairs, that the forest fire was as yet only a threat to the house and that her exit would not be blocked.

The rapidly approaching flames, teased by the wind, leapt to attack the living room windows, shattering them, numbing her brain so that instinct alone guided her bare feet along the fireplace wall, past the still ringing telephone, which had awakened her just in time. Please, please let it be in time.

Frenziedly she wrestled with the bolt on the door. Normally it slid back easily, but she was impeded by the smoke and the scorching heat—the bolt itself felt intensely hot—and her own fumbling fingers. Several agonising moments later she was beginning to think she would never get out. She banged the door in futile desperation. She heard the, by this time, familiar sound of splintering glass; then a voice said: 'You're all right, my love. I'm here.' And she fell, laughing and crying, into Ian's arms.

He had entered by way of the pantry window, set in the gable end. Quickly, effortlessly, he dealt with the bolt and then, his arm anchoring her nightgown clad form, he half walked, half carried her outside.

The scene of unusual activity, already several fire brigades had arrived and were pressing into action, took on the unreality of a dream. She couldn't remember Ian stripping off his jacket, but she could feel the warmth of it round her shoulders, and she was no longer barefoot but wearing a pair of masculine brogues, size: enormous.

She was gulping fresh air in a distraught, undignified manner. Ian was saying something to the effect of: 'Val . . . must go in and get Val.' Her brain roused itself to say sluggishly: 'Not . . . in . . . bed empty.' Then she was suddenly alert, uttering a heartfelt: 'Don't leave me. Please don't go back in there.'

The yard was full of flitting people, a confusion of voices, making an indistinguishable mumbo-jumbo of noise, a babble, a deafening roar. She wanted to stop up her ears. Ian . . . where was Ian? Gone, heedless of his own safety, intent on saving Val.

She tugged at someone's sleeve. 'The house? Will the house catch fire?'

The reply was given, but she didn't hear it. She swayed and fell into a deep faint.

*   *   *

She was in hospital again. An impersonal voice said: 'How do you feel?'

'Like a cup of tea,' decided Karen.

'Before or after?'

'Before or after what?'

'I show in your visitor. How about as well as? I'm sure you could both do with a cup.'

With extra sugar, please nurse. Good for shock,' said a familiar, exquisitely dear voice. 'Ian,' she welcomed. 'Help! I bet I look a sight! Come in and tell me the worst.' His fingers curled round hers, warming her cold heart. In her joy at seeing him, whole and unharmed, she didn't notice that his eyes were full of shadows.

'How are you?' he asked.

'Fine. I had to have five stitches in my arm. Flying glass, you know. And three somewhere else. I earned those running away, if you please!'

'A blow to your dignity?' he suggested delicately, but his amusement was so obviously a pretence, and not an award winning one at that, that she knew something was badly wrong. Had he had to stand helplessly by and watch the house go up in flames? It would be a blow, but it would not annihilate him. He had been the one to tell her that possessions count for nothing. Only people matter. 'Oh my darling' cried her heart. 'What is it? Tell me, let me help.'

'The house,' she began tentatively. 'Is it—?'

'No. The firemen did a marvellous job. Every pane of glass is broken and it needs a major decoration job. Nothing that time and money can't put right.'

'Oh, Ian. I'm so glad. But—?' If it wasn't the house. Then what—?

'Val,' he said, his face a grief-stricken mask. 'Val turned up after they took you to hospital.'

'Oh? She wasn't in the house, then? I wondered about that, although I didn't see how she could be. Because surely I would have stumbled over her, or something.'

He said nothing, just continued to look as if all the stuffing had been knocked out of him. Her brain latched on to an idea, played it; it fitted into a groove like a well worn record. It must have been running through her mind all the time.

'You don't have to tell me, Ian. I think I know. Val started the fire, didn't she? She hated the forest, although I didn't realize how intensely until now. Did she mean the house to catch fire?'

'It's a possibility.'

'Don't be too hard on her,' she pleaded. 'She loved the house as much as she hated the forest. I suppose she couldn't bear the thought

191

of us loving it and living there, happily together. But she regretted her action.'

'What makes you think that?' She noticed his eyes. There was such a look of hope in them that it wrung her dry. If Val had had a change of heart, even at the last moment, it somehow wouldn't be as bad.

'I know I'm right. The phone was ringing, remember? It was Val, ringing to warn me. It could only be her. She wanted to save my life. Ian, we mustn't blame her. Don't you see, she is sicker than either of us realized. We must help her all we can.'

'Bless you.' His mouth tightened and the nerve under his left eye jumped.

'Val doesn't need our help any more. You see, after telephoning, if she did, we can only theorise on that point, she came back. She was seen entering the forest. Several people went in after her, but it was hopeless. Within seconds the path she took was impassable. She was swallowed whole.'

Oh my love, no, no, no! How awful you must feel. What can I do, how best can I share your pain? Not only your pain, I was beginning to understand Val, understand her and like her.

'Swallowed whole. Odd you should use that expression. It's what she felt . . . perhaps she sensed it would happen. If she did, if she really saw into the future, it must have been a happy release. The actual moment can have been nothing to the agony of waiting. Poor . . . stricken . . . Val! Poor old you.'

He said: 'I'll get over it. I just feel as if I've failed her in some way.'

'Don't talk like that. No one could have done more.' She couldn't bear to see him looking so gaunt, so grimly devoid of hope, or feeling, or anything. She must say something to take his mind off this tragic thing. She must make him look forward.

'About us?' How warily she must tread. 'Or is it too soon to ask?' It was working. He looked less bleak, warmer somehow.

'It's never too soon to start planning for the future. Life must go on.' And yet, even as he spoke, she wondered if he could bear to remain in the village after all that had happened. It would wrench her heart to leave Hamblewick, but if he wanted to leave she would go with him willingly.

But when she said as much, he smiled a tender ghost of a smile, and promised to remember only the happy times. 'There is just one thing,' he said, his tone slightly pensive. 'It might take some time to put the house in order, and we seem to have wasted such a lot of time already. And,'—his fingers tightened on hers—'my quarters haven't suffered any damage at all. So, my darling, do you fancy starting married life in one room over a garage?'

'Plus kitchenette,' she said huskily. 'Stop

offering me Paradise.'

Contentedly, happily, she went into his arms.

We hope you have enjoyed this Large Print book. Other Chivers Press or Thorndike Press Large Print books are available at your library or directly from the publishers.

For more information about current and forthcoming titles, please call or write, without obligation, to:

Chivers Large Print
published by BBC Audiobooks Ltd
St James House, The Square
Lower Bristol Road
Bath BA2 3BH
UK
email: bbcaudiobooks@bbc.co.uk
www.bbcaudiobooks.co.uk

OR

Thorndike Press
295 Kennedy Memorial Drive
Waterville
Maine 04901
USA
www.gale.com/thorndike
www.gale.com/wheeler

All our Large Print titles are designed for easy reading, and all our books are made to last.